"OK, guys, let's get psyched!" Jessica said on Tuesday afternoon at practice. "We've got three days to get in shape for nationals. We looked great at State, and we're going to look even better in Yosemite."

Jessica was determined to get the squad back on track. She and Heather had called for double practices all week, and the practice session that morning had been disastrous. The girls had wasted the entire morning trying to imitate Heather's combination jump—at Heather's suggestion, of course. Heather knew perfectly well that the other girls wouldn't be able to do it. It was just another opportunity for her to show off. But Jessica was determined not to waste any more time. She wasn't going to let Heather undermine her authority any further.

"V" FOR VICTORY

Written by
Kate William

Created by
FRANCINE PASCAL

BANTAM BOOKS
NEW YORK·TORONTO·LONDON·SYDNEY·AUCKLAND

RL 6, age 12 and up

"V" FOR VICTORY

A Bantam Book / March 1995

Sweet Valley High® is a registered trademark of Francine Pascal
Conceived by Francine Pascal
Produced by Daniel Weiss Associates, Inc.
33 West 17th Street
New York, NY 10011
Cover art by Bruce Emmett

ISBN: 0-553-56632-6

Published simultaneously in the United States and Canada

Bantam Books are published by Bantam Books, a division of Bantam
Doubleday Dell Publishing Group, Inc. Its trademark, consisting of the
words "Bantam Books" and the portrayal of a rooster, is Registered in
U.S. Patent and Trademark Office and in other countries. Marca
Registrada. Bantam Books, 1540 Broadway, New York, New York 10036.

PRINTED IN THE UNITED STATES OF AMERICA

OPM   0 9 8 7 6 5 4 3 2

To Anders Johansson

Chapter 1

"I don't think I can take another minute of this!" Jessica Wakefield exclaimed on Saturday afternoon, her body tense with anticipation as the awards ceremony of the State Cheerleading Championships in Santa Barbara reached its climax. Jessica and her squad at Sweet Valley High were competing at State for the first time, and it looked as if they had a chance to take home the title.

"I know," whispered Amy Sutton, her slate-gray eyes flashing with excitement. "I think I'm going to explode."

"Well, at least it's finally show time," Jessica said, tightening her blond ponytail on top of her head and adjusting her sunglasses. They'd been sitting in the hot afternoon sun for nearly an hour while a series of merit awards were distributed. Now only the winning squads remained to be announced.

"Attention, everybody!" called Victoria Knox, the state representative of the American Cheerleading Association. "The ACA is proud to present the top three cheerleading squads in the state of California. We recognize these squads as representing excellence in all cheerleading categories, including athletic ability, artistic impression, and most important, school spirit. And now the envelope, please!"

The girls fidgeted nervously as an athletic-looking young woman in blue nylon shorts and a white T-shirt ran out onto the field. "Thank you." Ms. Knox smiled as the woman handed her an oversize envelope. She cupped her hand around the microphone and spoke into it. "Please hold your applause until all the teams have been named."

"Why don't they just get on with it?" complained Lila Fowler, swinging her heavy mane of long brown hair over her shoulders.

"Lila, shh!" said Jessica, straining to hear Ms. Knox's voice.

"For their flawless execution and athletic prowess, the third-place award goes to Sacramento High," announced Ms. Knox, holding up a small copper trophy in the shape of a cheerleader.

The audience remained quiet, but the Sacramento squad let out an enthusiastic shout.

Amy leaned over to Jessica. "I can't believe it," she breathed. "Sacramento came in third!"

Jessica flashed her an optimistic smile and held up crossed fingers. The Sacramento squad had seemed like their most imposing opponent. The

2

girls from Sacramento had put on an extremely impressive athletic performance, finishing with a spectacular display of team jumps. "Maybe their routine was too technical," whispered Jessica to Amy.

Ms. Knox's voice boomed out across the field. "And for impressive tumbling, innovative choreography, and an abundance of spirit, the second place winner is—"

Jessica held her breath as Ms. Knox fumbled with the envelope, praying her school wouldn't be named. "Laguna High from Laguna Beach, California! Girls, please come onto the field to accept your awards."

"We're going to win!" Jessica whispered excitedly to Lila, her cheeks flushed with excitement as the captains of the placing squads ran onto the field.

"La-di-da!" said Lila, twirling a red-and-white pom-pom in the air.

Jessica rolled her eyes. "You could at least pretend you're excited," she said. She knew that Lila had agreed to be on the squad only because she was Jessica's best friend. Lila had been on the team a long time ago, but she had quit, claiming that cheerleading was a boring, useless activity.

"Well, this is it, guys!" squealed Annie Whitman, her green eyes sparkling. "It's all or nothing now."

Patty Gilbert, Jade Wu, and Sara Eastbourne, all talented dancers, took up a quiet cheer. "SVH! SVH! SVH!" they intoned together.

Jessica looked around at her squad as the others

3

picked up the cheer, chanting softly and clapping rhythmically. All the girls were caught up in the excitement of the moment. Sandy Bacon and her best friend, Jean West, were huddled together, holding on to each other for support. Maria Santelli and Annie Whitman were tapping on the bleachers in time with the cheer. Even her twin sister, Elizabeth, seemed to be sharing in the enthusiasm. Jessica felt a swell of pride as she took in the squad she had put together. They had performed to perfection this afternoon, she thought with satisfaction, and they deserved to win.

Jessica held her breath as the announcer ripped open the envelope containing the first-place winners. A drumroll began from the far end of the field, and Jessica could feel her heart beating in time with it. "And now," intoned Ms. Knox, speaking in an enticingly slow voice, "the—number one—cheerleading squad—in the entire state of California is . . . Sweet Valley High!"

The crowd roared and jumped up spontaneously. Jessica was elated, swept up in the excitement as she was pulled up to her feet with the crowd. "C'mon, guys!" Jessica exclaimed, waving to her teammates to follow her down the bleachers. Jessica felt a rush of energy as the girls ran across the field, waving their pom-poms in the air. She almost couldn't believe it was true. Her squad had won the state championships! They were better than all of the cheerleading squads in California! They were going to nationals for the first time ever!

4

Suddenly her cocaptain, Heather Mallone, shoved past her and sprinted to the podium ahead of the rest of the girls. For a moment Jessica had forgotten that she had to share her glory with her archrival, the beautiful new girl in town who had taken over her squad and was trying to take over the entire school. *How typical,* thought Jessica, wondering what kind of stunt Heather was going to pull.

"Congratulations," said Ms. Knox, holding out a gold statuette as Heather reached the podium, the other girls behind her. Heather accepted the trophy graciously as warm applause filled the stadium. Jessica steamed as she watched Heather grab the microphone and stand poised in the middle of the field, waiting for the crowd to settle down. *She's just basking in the attention, isn't she?* thought Jessica to herself bitterly.

Heather cleared her throat and flashed a big-toothed white smile at the audience. "I just want to thank everybody on my squad for all their hard work," she said, flipping her blond hair with a shake of her head.

My squad! thought Jessica in indignation. *She* was the official captain of the squad. *She* was the one who had carried her squad through weeks and weeks of training the entire year. Heather had been cocaptain for only a few weeks. "Can you believe her?" whispered Jessica to Amy in indignation.

"Jessica, please," said Amy. "This isn't the time to sharpen your claws." She turned her attention

5

back to Heather, a rapturous smile plastered on her face. Jessica gritted her teeth, seething in frustration.

"But most of all, I want to thank *you*," continued Heather in her annoyingly sexy voice, extending her hand in a gracious gesture, "you—the judges, the audience, and our friends, for recognizing my squad for what it is—the best in the state and soon to be the best in the nation!"

Jessica's face burned as the crowd cheered in appreciation. All the Sweet Valley High cheerleaders were crowded around the podium, jumping and screaming. Jessica couldn't believe it. Was the entire squad blind? She moved forward to take the mike and make a speech of her own when the roar of the crowd interrupted her.

"Com-bo jump! Com-bo jump!" yelled the audience, calling for a replay of Heather's famous combination jump, the jump with which they had finished their routine.

Jessica stared aghast as Heather put on a dazzling solo display. She performed her combination jump with aplomb, pulling off a flawless triple herky and Y-leap combination. Then she ran across the field and performed a series of back flips, finishing off with a perfect landing in the splits.

"Bravo! Bravo!" yelled the crowd, hooting and cheering for more. Jessica couldn't stand one more moment of Heather's sickening display. She slipped away from the circle of cheering girls and darted across the field toward the goalpost. She looked back to see if anybody had noticed her leave, but the girls seemed oblivious, completely entranced with the nauseating spectacle Heather was making of herself.

Well, victory isn't as sweet as I imagined, Jessica thought, ducking into the deserted gym. She couldn't stand sharing the spotlight with Heather. *Sharing it!* thought Jessica wryly as she made her way across the stadium. *Having it stolen right out from under me is more like it.* She almost wished they had lost just so she could have seen Heather humiliated.

Ever since beautiful blond Heather Mallone had stepped into the Dairi Burger, she'd been making Jessica's life a living nightmare. Heather had apparently been the big star of the cheerleading squad at her old high school, Thomas Jefferson High, in Reno, Nevada. And she had decided to be the star of her *new* school as well, thought Jessica with annoyance. She had arrived on the scene at exactly the same time that Jessica's old cocaptain, Robin Wilson, had moved out of town. Not only had the girls voted unanimously to let Heather join the squad, but they had voted her in as cocaptain as well.

That's when everything started falling apart. Heather had taken over the squad like an army invading foreign territory—she had introduced new cheers, new uniforms, and even a new diet-and-exercise program. And the girls had eaten it up. Even though the uniforms were cheap and skimpy, the diet unrealistic, and the exercise plan like a military regime, the girls had followed her every step

7

of the way—all because she promised to lead them to nationals. She had undercut Jessica's authority at every turn, making Jessica look like the enemy and turning all the girls against her.

Jessica seethed as she ticked off Heather's offenses in her mind. One day at practice while Jessica was sick at home, Heather had even had the audacity to fire Maria and Sandy, two of the most seasoned girls on the squad. Heather's irritating, singsong voice rang in her head. *"We all have to make sacrifices for the good of the team,"* she had said. Jessica had tried to rally the girls around her, but they had all stood behind Heather's decision to let Maria and Sandy go. Then, at the big game against Claremont, Heather had led the girls in a cheer that Jessica didn't even know. Jessica had just stood on the sidelines, humiliated, while her team pranced and cheered without her. That had been the last straw. "I quit!" Jessica had yelled, throwing down her pom-poms and flouncing off the field.

But Jessica Wakefield wasn't one to sit on the sidelines for long. So she had organized a squad of her own, recruiting her best friend, her sister, and a number of dancers at school. With a week of intense practice, she had put together a stellar squad, a squad that turned out to be so good, the American Cheerleading Association representative recommended combining the two squads for the state competition. She had Ken Matthews to thank for that. It had all been his idea.

Ken, thought Jessica glumly, walking out of the

silent gym and blinking at the bright sunlight. She sat down under a tree, feeling dejected despite the squad's victory. She felt as if she had lost everything that mattered to her. Not only had Heather stolen her squad, but her own sister, Elizabeth, had stolen her boyfriend.

Jessica had been thrilled to be dating handsome blond Ken Matthews, the well-built captain and quarterback of the Gladiators, the Sweet Valley High football team. She had expected her sister to be happy for her, too, but Elizabeth had been strangely pessimistic about the whole thing. She had kept warning Jessica to go slowly, and every chance she got, she had discouraged her being with Ken. It almost seemed as if she were trying to undermine their relationship.

And then one day Jessica discovered why. She was in Elizabeth's room when she happened upon a series of framed photos of Ken and Elizabeth in a photo booth—kissing. Driven by curiosity, Jessica had hunted out her sister's journal, only to discover that Ken and Elizabeth had had a secret fling while Elizabeth's longtime boyfriend and Ken's best friend, Todd Wilkins, was living in Vermont.

Jessica hadn't minded at first. She was surprised that Elizabeth had been so secretive about the whole thing, but it was all in the past. Ken was interested in her, and not her sister, now. But Elizabeth wasn't content with letting the past be the past. She wanted Ken back, and she wasn't going to let anything stop her. She had even gone so far as to pull a twin switch, going out on a date with Ken disguised as Jessica. Ken had fixed a romantic picnic, and they had shared a kiss at the beach. Ken hadn't even realized it was Elizabeth until he'd kissed her. Jessica's face blazed with the memory. How could Elizabeth have betrayed her like that? How could Ken have confused them?

Elizabeth Wakefield, her face creased with concern, watched Jessica run off the field. She jumped up to follow her but checked herself, remembering that she and Jessica weren't speaking.

"We did it!" yelled Annie Whitman, grabbing Maria Santelli around the waist and spinning her around.

"We're numero uno!" agreed Maria with a happy smile as Annie flung her in a circle.

Elizabeth backed away from the circle of girls hugging and congratulating each other. She was happy for the squad, but she couldn't care less about nationals. In fact, it was all a big pain. She had agreed to be on the squad in the first place only because Jessica had blackmailed her. After Jessica had discovered the truth about Elizabeth and Ken's fling, she had threatened to tell Todd everything if Elizabeth refused to be on her new squad. Elizabeth had hoped the squad would go to regionals, lose, and be done with it. Who would have thought they'd get this far?

"Hea-ther! Hea-ther!" yelled the girls, making a seat with their hands and lifting her in the air.

"Hey, Jessica, c'mon, you're the cocaptain!" shouted Annie, turning toward Elizabeth.

"What?" said Elizabeth, facing her with a startled expression on her face.

"C'mon, you guys, let's get Jess," said Annie to Maria and Sandy. "After all, there are two heroes here."

"No, no, I'm Elizabeth!" Elizabeth cried as the girls heaved her onto their shoulders. She struggled and tried to protest again, but the din of the crowd drowned her out.

Elizabeth sighed and relaxed, realizing she would have to ride it out. She forced a grin on her face, waving stiffly at the crowds as the girls carried her and Heather across the field.

"Jes-si-ca! Jes-si-ca!" yelled the girls, bouncing her in the air. Singing at the top of their lungs, they broke out into a round of "For She's a Jolly Good Fellow."

Elizabeth was mortified. Everybody could always tell her and Jessica apart. How could the girls have confused them? Jessica and Elizabeth might look identical, from their long golden-blond hair to their sparkling blue eyes to the matching dimples in their left cheeks, but that was where the similarities ended. In their styles and personality they were completely different. Jessica was on the wild side. She always wore funky clothes and tried out outrageous new hairstyles. Her look reflected her personality: Jessica liked to be seen. Jessica was happy as long as she was the center of the action, whether it be the center of a party, the center of a shopping mall, or the center of a beach. Elizabeth, on the other hand, preferred the periphery. While

11

Elizabeth liked having fun as much as her sister, she was more academic and socially minded. Elizabeth wrote a weekly column for *The Oracle*, the Sweet Valley High newspaper, and spent much of her spare time with her boyfriend, Todd Wilkins, or her best friend, Enid Rollins. Elizabeth was more conservative than her sister, preferring to wear comfortable clothing, her hair pulled back in a ponytail. From one look at them, from their styles to their demeanor, you could always tell them apart.

Well, thought Elizabeth as the girls paraded her and Heather across the field, *lately I have been acting more like Jessica than myself.* Not only did she *look* like Jessica in her cheerleading attire, but she'd been acting like her too. When Jessica had started dating Ken Matthews, Elizabeth had been consumed with jealousy. She had found herself acting completely out of character—wishing the worst for her sister, hoping she didn't enjoy herself, trying to sabotage her sister's dates.

And then she had pulled an uncharacteristically manipulative move. In a misguided effort to resolve her feelings for Ken, Elizabeth had disguised herself as Jessica and had gone out with him. Fortunately, when they had kissed, there had been no spark. Elizabeth had discovered then and there that the only person she wanted to be kissing was Todd. Ken had realized at the same moment that he was kissing Elizabeth, not Jessica. Elizabeth had explained everything, and Ken had been very understanding. They both had decided to go straight to Todd's to come clean about the fling they'd had when Todd was living in Vermont. But when she and Ken had driven up to Todd's house, they had found that Jessica had beaten them to it. Jessica had discovered Elizabeth's ploy and had driven straight over to Todd's, Elizabeth's diary in hand. Neither Jessica nor Todd had given them a chance to explain. Todd had broken up with her then and there. And she and Jessica hadn't spoken since. Elizabeth had never felt so alone in her life.

Finally Elizabeth saw the bleachers come into sight again. She heaved a sigh of relief as the girls deposited her onto the field. She had always known that she didn't want to be the center of attention, but this clinched it. Suddenly her face blanched as she noticed Jessica standing by the bleachers waiting for them, her arms crossed stiffly across her chest.

"Jessica!" Elizabeth exclaimed, speechless.

"What's wrong, Liz?" said Jessica, fire in her eyes. "It's not enough to steal my boyfriend, but you've got to steal my glory too?"

Elizabeth turned to face her, sputtering. "You . . . you don't understand," she said. But Jessica was already stomping across the field, her blond ponytail swishing behind her.

Chapter 2

"So tell us all about it, Elizabeth!" said Mrs. Wakefield brightly on Monday morning, setting down on the butcher-block table a bowl of granola and yogurt adorned with fresh strawberries. She laid a plateful of warm blueberry muffins next to it. In her pale-pink linen suit, Alice Wakefield looked as crisp and fresh as the balmy California day.

"About what?" mumbled Elizabeth, her nose stuck in her orange-juice glass.

"About your victory at State on Saturday!" Mrs. Wakefield said, pulling up a chair and giving Elizabeth her full attention.

"Oh, well, we won," muttered Elizabeth, averting her eyes. Her mother was acting especially chipper this morning, she thought, bustling around the sunny Wakefield kitchen preparing breakfast. Elizabeth usually appreciated her mother's good humor, but this morning she wasn't in the mood

14

for it. She felt blacker than the bitter black coffee she was drinking.

"That's quite an achievement, isn't it?" said Mr. Wakefield, picking up the bowl of granola and serving them all. "The cheerleaders have never even gone to State before, right?"

"Quite an achievement," muttered Elizabeth sarcastically. "Winning the Nobel Peace Prize, that's an achievement. Being awarded the Purple Heart for bravery, that's an achievement. Winning a Pulitzer Prize, that's an achievement. Cheerleading? That's stupid."

"Elizabeth!" said Mrs. Wakefield sharply.

Elizabeth looked down at the table. Her outburst was completely out of character. "I'm sorry," she said, tears filling her eyes. *That was completely unnecessary,* Elizabeth thought, berating herself. Usually she could put up a pretty good front when things weren't going right, but today it didn't seem to be working. Elizabeth was dreading the day ahead. She was sure to come across Todd at school, and she had to face Jessica at cheerleading practice. The two people she loved most in the world weren't speaking to her, and it was all her fault. Tears clouded her vision again, and Elizabeth ducked her head, pressing a napkin to her eyes.

"That's all right, sweetie," said Mrs. Wakefield, patting her hand and looking at her with concern.

"Where's Jessica?" asked Mr. Wakefield, changing the subject abruptly. "Isn't she going to be late for school?"

15

"She's probably getting her beauty sleep," said Elizabeth wryly.

Just then Jessica came careening into the room, her sunglasses in hand and her book bag flung over her shoulder. "Hey, Mom, have you seen my pom-poms?" she asked in a rush.

Jessica looked particularly striking, thought Elizabeth. She was wearing a floral-print teal baby-doll dress that brought out the sparkle in her blue-green eyes and accentuated her honey-blond hair. *She's probably spent hours this morning preparing for all the attention she'll get at school today,* thought Elizabeth.

"They're in the den, dear," said Mrs. Wakefield tolerantly, "where you left them yesterday."

"Good morning, Dad," Jessica said, pointedly ignoring Elizabeth.

"Morning, sweetheart," Mr. Wakefield answered. Jessica grabbed a muffin for the road and ran out of the room. "See you later!" she called.

A few minutes later Elizabeth could hear Jessica rev the engine and pull away in the twins' Jeep. Usually Jessica and Elizabeth shared a ride to school, but ever since the incident with Ken, Jessica had taken to leaving without her.

"Well, Mom," Elizabeth said with a sigh, "it looks like you'll have to give me a ride to school on your way to work again."

"Drama-club member Bill Chase encountered high drama at Bridgewater's Shakespeare Festival last weekend," read Elizabeth, murmuring to herself as she skimmed the contents of her article on the computer screen. It was Monday after school and Elizabeth was at the *Oracle* office, putting the final touches on her "Personal Profiles" column for the week. She sat back and gnawed on a fingernail, thinking of an appropriate conclusion. "A dramatic finish to a dramatic event," she typed in quickly, adding the final period with a flourish. Elizabeth scrolled up and scanned the entire article quickly. Satisfied with the results, she pressed "save" and "print."

"Here you go, Penny," Elizabeth said, pulling the article from the printer and handing it to Penny Ayala, the lanky, fair-haired editor in chief of the newspaper and a good friend of Elizabeth's.

"Thanks, Liz," said Penny warmly, taking the page from her. She whistled softly as she perused the article. "Wow, you sure are on the ball. We don't need this until Wednesday."

"I know," said Elizabeth, "but I'm going to be busy with cheerleading practice all week." She made a face and Penny laughed. "In fact," Elizabeth said, glancing down at her watch, "I've got to run or I'm going to be late."

Elizabeth swung her book bag over her shoulder and rushed to the door.

"Whoa!" said a laughing voice.

"Mr. Collins!" Elizabeth exclaimed as she collided with the newspaper's faculty adviser at the door. She jumped out of his way quickly. "Sorry!" she said.

"That's all right, no harm done," said Mr. Collins

good-naturedly, walking into the office and dropping his briefcase on a chair. He rubbed his right arm. "I didn't really need this arm, anyway," he joked.

Elizabeth smiled. Mr. Collins always managed to cheer her up. Not only was Mr. Collins Elizabeth's favorite English teacher, but she considered him a friend as well.

"Actually, Liz, I'm glad I bumped into you," said Mr. Collins.

"And you did bump into me!" quipped Elizabeth.

Mr. Collins grinned as he popped open his briefcase. He rummaged through the papers and pulled out a list of story assignments. "Listen, Liz, I've got a favor to ask you."

"Sure," Elizabeth said amenably, hopping up on a stool by the drafting table. "Shoot."

"I need someone to write the front-page story for the upcoming edition, and we're a little shorthanded," explained Mr. Collins. "Olivia Davidson was supposed to write the coverage, but she's at home sick. And John Pfeifer is out on a sports beat, covering the tennis-team championships."

"I'd be happy to write the story," said Elizabeth agreeably. "When do you need it?"

"Actually, it's a bit of a rush," said Mr. Collins, an apologetic expression on his face. "We need to get the paper to press this afternoon."

Elizabeth calculated quickly. She could probably crank out the article in half an hour. With any luck the girls would probably still be limbering up when she arrived at the athletic field. She'd miss the warm-up exercises, but she'd be there in time for practice.

"So do you think you can manage it?" asked Mr. Collins, looking at her anxiously.

Elizabeth nodded. "Sure, no problem," she said.

"Great, great," said Mr. Collins, looking visibly relieved. "The article's a feature story on the cheerleading victory at State this weekend."

Elizabeth's jaw dropped. "The cheerleading victory at State?" she repeated.

"That's right," said Mr. Collins. "In fact, now that you've joined the squad, you're the perfect person to cover it." He patted her on the shoulder and walked away.

Elizabeth groaned as she headed back to the computer. She could easily envision what the story should be: a peppy, spirited article full of cheerleading puns and school spirit. She just couldn't imagine herself writing it.

Elizabeth flicked on the computer and stared at the blank screen, trying to summon the energy to write the appropriate coverage. What was there to say? she wondered. The SVH cheerleading squad went to State and they won. Finis, end of story. *OK, just get down the basic facts*, Elizabeth encouraged herself. *Start at the beginning.* She concentrated on the journalistic convention of packing all the newsworthy information into the first line. Who? The cheerleaders. What? The state championship. Where? Santa Barbara. When? Saturday. Why? She couldn't imagine.

Writing about cheerleading was even harder than doing it, thought Elizabeth with a sigh. She wouldn't have had such a problem writing a cheerleading article the week before. When Jessica had first coerced her into joining the squad, Elizabeth had been miserable. The thought of jumping around in a silly little skirt made her stomach turn. But then she found herself getting into it despite herself. She had actually enjoyed the challenge of preparing for the state championship. But now she was sick of it, and fighting with Jessica had taken every bit of the fun out of it.

Elizabeth put her head in her hands. Why did Mr. Collins have to assign her this story, of all things? Then she shook herself and sat upright, forcing herself to tackle the first line. "In an unprecedented event the Sweet Valley High cheerleading squad, cocaptained by Jessica Wakefield and Heather Mallone, championed a first-place victory at the state championships on Saturday at Santa Barbara." Hmm, this wasn't so hard, Elizabeth thought, continuing to type. "The cheerleaders will be competing in the national championship in Yosemite next weekend."

Forty-five minutes later Elizabeth was still sitting in front of the screen. She had managed to get down the basic facts, but she couldn't seem to infuse the article with the enthusiasm it warranted. Now she was almost an hour late for practice. Elizabeth felt like tearing her hair out. "I give up," she said finally, throwing up her hands. She quickly typed in a title—"V for Victory"—and printed out the article.

"Penny!" Elizabeth called. "Do you think you could help me out here for a minute?"

"Sure, one sec!" Penny said, crouched on the floor in front of a full-page spread. She carefully laid out the final photograph, smoothing it down with the back of her hand. Then she jumped up and joined Elizabeth.

"Penny, I need your help," said Elizabeth, raking a hand through her hair. "I'm writing this feature story about cheerleading that needs to get out today, and I've got to get to cheerleading practice. The story is late—no, *I'm* late, and I can't seem to get the cheerleading spirit into my practice—I mean, my story." She stopped, confused.

"OK, slow down and take a deep breath," Penny instructed. Elizabeth breathed in deeply, trying to calm herself.

"Now, start all over," Penny said. "What's the problem?"

"The problem is that I haven't finished this State cheerleading story and I'm late for practice. I've got down the basic facts, but it's lacking any flair—you know, school-spirit stuff," explained Elizabeth. "Do you think you could just add the finishing touches?"

"Consider it done!" said Penny, taking the article out of her hand. "I'd be happy to spice it up a bit."

"Penny, are you sure?" asked Elizabeth, biting her lip.

"Of course!" said Penny, taking a seat in front of the computer. She made a shooing motion with her hand. "Now get out of here!"

21

"Thanks, Penny," Elizabeth said, smiling gratefully. "I owe you one!"

"Just don't bang up your hands flipping," said Penny. "We need you here!"

I can't seem to do anything right these days, sighed Elizabeth as she flew into the girls' locker room to change into her cheerleading-practice attire. She had always prided herself on her work at the newspaper. Elizabeth never shirked her duty. No matter how tight the deadline, she always managed to complete her assignments. It was a commonplace around the office that in a crisis Elizabeth was the woman to get the job done. Usually she found herself taking up the slack, finishing up other people's work. But this time she'd had to pass her article off on Penny. And she was still late for cheerleading practice— over an hour late.

Jessica will probably think I'm late on purpose, thought Elizabeth as she slammed her locker door shut. But it was probably just as well that she missed the beginning of practice, she reasoned, trying to reassure herself. That way she wouldn't have to worry about talking—or not talking—to her sister.

When Elizabeth finally arrived in the gym in her cheerleading attire, however, the girls hadn't yet begun to practice. They were sitting together in a circle on the floor.

"Hi, Elizabeth!" Sandy Bacon and Jean West waved. Maria Santelli patted a place on the floor

22

by her side for Elizabeth to sit down. Elizabeth smiled weakly and took a seat next to her.

"Oh, Liz, how gracious of you to show up," Jessica said sarcastically.

"Sorry," Elizabeth said. "I got held up at *The Oracle*."

"Well, you're going to have to rearrange your priorities if you plan to stay on the team," said Jessica in a patronizing tone.

Elizabeth gritted her teeth. As if she had any interest in staying on the team! She felt like screaming out for everyone to hear: "If you weren't blackmailing me, I wouldn't come near your stupid squad!" But of course Elizabeth couldn't say anything. Jessica had her over a barrel.

"Well," said Jessica, standing up. "Now that we're all *finally* here . . ." Emphasizing each word for Elizabeth's benefit, she paused meaningfully. "I guess we can begin."

Elizabeth was horrified. Had Jessica made the team wait an entire hour just to show her up? She felt a blush crawl slowly up her neck to her cheeks. "Were you all waiting for me?" Elizabeth whispered worriedly to Maria.

Maria shook her head emphatically. "Don't worry," she reassured her. "Jessica and Heather have been having a little debate."

Elizabeth raised her eyebrows and looked at her quizzically. "About costumes," Maria said, rolling her eyes.

Elizabeth couldn't help grinning.

"Do you mind?" said Jessica, glaring at both

of them. "We have business to take care of."

"Sorry, sorry," mumbled Elizabeth and Maria.

"Thank you!" Jessica said curtly. "Now, as you know, the national competition is being held in California this year—in Yosemite. I have just received the official roster of all the teams competing." She held up a piece of paper rolled up like a scroll. "I'll read off the names so we know what we're up against." Jessica unfurled the list and began to read aloud when Heather swiped it out of the air.

"Lemme see that!" Heather snarled.

Elizabeth was surprised at Heather's obvious aggressiveness. Heather usually hid her real motives behind a candy-coated smile and a gracious veneer. Jessica thought Heather was a calculating witch, and Elizabeth tended to agree with her. When Heather had first arrived, Elizabeth had tried to give her a chance. Heather had seemed like a very interesting and talented girl with a genuine love for cheerleading. Elizabeth had thought Jessica was just jealous of all the attention the new girl was receiving.

But after Heather had taken over the cheerleading squad, Elizabeth had changed her mind. First Heather had fired Maria and Sandy behind Jessica's back. Then she had slowly usurped Jessica's authority, finally causing her to quit her own squad. Heather might have a genuine goal to make the Sweet Valley High cheerleaders the best in the country, thought Elizabeth, but she didn't care whom she hurt in the process.

"Hey!" said Jessica, and tried to grab the list back, but Heather was oblivious. She was furiously scanning the list. Suddenly her face went white.

"Look! Thomas Jefferson High in Reno," exclaimed Amy Sutton, who had been reading over her shoulder. "That's your old team, Heather!"

"Of course it's my old team. Don't you think I know that?" snapped Heather.

An uncomfortable silence greeted her strange response. Amy coughed nervously and a few of the girls looked to Jessica for guidance.

Jessica shrugged and stared at Heather, her arms folded across her chest.

"Well," said Heather a moment later, pulling herself together, "I guess that somehow they're managing without me."

"I can't imagine how," said Jessica snidely, grabbing the list back from Heather and continuing to read aloud. "Brattleboro, Burlington, Evanston High, Hartford, Little Rock, Pawtucket, Riverdale, Tampa Bay . . ."

Elizabeth watched the exchange with interest. Heather still seemed to look a little blanched. *Something's up here,* Elizabeth thought, her reporter's nose sensing trouble.

"Well, another episode of the Jessica-Heather saga comes to a close," said Lila to Amy as she steered her lime-green Triumph into the parking lot of the Dairi Burger, Sweet Valley's most popular teen hangout. The girls had accomplished practically nothing at practice. Jessica and Heather couldn't agree on which cheers to practice, and they had finally given up and just discussed logistics concerning nationals. The girls had decided to stop in at the Dairi Burger for burgers and shakes to wind down after practice.

"The soap opera continues," said Amy, jumping out of the car and slamming the door. "Tune in next week for the rousing conclusion to our six-part miniseries: Jessica and Heather at the national competition."

Lila laughed and then shook her head ruefully. "If those two don't get it together," she said, "we're going to be the laughingstock of the competition."

"I know," Amy agreed as she crossed the lot with Lila.

"I never realized how competitive cheerleading is," Lila remarked. "I always thought cheerleaders just stood on the sidelines."

"Not around here, that's for sure," said Amy, running her fingers through her long blond hair.

"Wow, check out the scene," said Lila as they reached the wooden door of the Dairi Burger. The restaurant was hopping, as usual. It seemed like everybody from Sweet Valley High had decided to stop in at the Dairi Burger after practice. Members of the girls' cheerleading squad as well as the boys' football and basketball teams were converging on the door at once.

"Hey, there's Jessica and Elizabeth," said Amy, pointing to the front of the room.

"And there's Todd and Ken," said Lila, raising her eyebrows.

Amy and Lila watched as Jessica and Elizabeth grabbed the same table by mistake. They both mumbled something unintelligible and quickly moved to separate tables. At the same time, Todd and Ken sat down together, then quickly got up and moved unwittingly to Jessica and Elizabeth's separate tables.

"Can you believe this?" said Lila, watching with a bemused smile as a Charlie Chaplin–like scene ensued.

"Jessica!" said Ken, a shocked expression on his face.

"If you'll excuse me," said Jessica, jumping up.

"Elizabeth!" said Todd, anger and hurt creasing his features. He quickly shoved back his chair.

"Oh, no, please allow me," said Elizabeth, holding out a hand.

All four of them stood up together. Elizabeth and Jessica quickly took their own booths, and Ken and Todd sat back down at the separate tables. Now Jessica, Elizabeth, Todd, and Ken had taken the only available tables in the restaurant.

"Well, there's nowhere left to sit now," said Lila, her arms folded across her chest. "It will sure make life easier for everybody when the Bobbsey twins and their boyfriends are on speaking terms again."

"Hi, everybody!" Heather exclaimed, waltzing into the restaurant as Jessica sat down alone in a booth.

"Hi, Heather!" returned some seniors from the girls' tennis team seated near the front of the restaurant. A bunch of admiring sophomore girls waved from a table. "Look, Heather's here!" somebody said.

"The queen appears," mumbled Jessica to herself as Heather made her grand entrance. Annie Whitman, who idolized Heather, was close on her tail. Jessica groaned inwardly as a few of the guys whistled appreciatively. "Lookin' good!" yelled Bruce Patman.

Heather stood by the door and swept the restaurant with a regal gaze, savoring the attention she was receiving. She walked through the crowd slowly, which seemed to part like the Red Sea to make way for her. Finally she stopped by Jessica's table.

"Well, it looks like the Wakefields, et al., have taken over the restaurant," said Heather in a loud, patronizing tone, "so we'll have to sit with Jessie here."

Jessica bristled at the name "Jessie" but didn't rise to the bait.

"Please do," said Jessica, putting on a huge smile. Heather and Annie piled into the seat across from Jessica.

Lila and Amy followed suit, sliding into the booth on Jessica's side.

"Hey, Jess," said Lila teasingly, "playing musical chairs again?"

"Yeah, it's a really fun game," responded Jessica sardonically.

Just then the waitress appeared. All of the girls ordered shakes—except for Heather, of course, who ordered her signature Diet Coke with lemon and a straw—and they got a few orders of fries for the table.

"I can't believe we're going to be competing against your old squad," said Annie to Heather excitedly. "I'll bet they're no good without you. You were the captain, right?"

Jessica feigned a huge yawn. "Do we have to go through all this again? Haven't we heard enough about Heather's illustrious cheerleading career?" She went on in a singsong voice. "Heather was the captain of the Thomas Jefferson cheerleading squad. Thomas Jefferson won State for ten years straight. Heather *personally* took her team to State for two years in a row, and they won both years all because of her fabulous combinations. Heather won the award for best cheerleader in Reno her sophomore year, and—"

"Jessica's right," Heather said, interrupting her. "That's all ancient history. Now, if you'll all excuse me, I have to study for the French quiz tomorrow."

"But Heather," Annie protested, "your Diet Coke—"

"I'm not really thirsty," said Heather, jumping up abruptly and throwing some bills onto the table. "See you all tomorrow at practice." She grabbed her gym bag and made her way to the door.

"Heather passed up an opportunity to brag?" said Jessica, shocked at Heather's uncharacteristic behavior. "She must have a fever!"

"Je veux, tu veux, il/elle veut," recited Elizabeth,

her French book open in front of her. "I want, you want, he/she wants. *Je veux, tu veux, il/elle veut*," she repeated. "*Je veux, je ne veux pas . . .*" Elizabeth's mind wandered off. *What I* want *is to have my sister and my boyfriend back,* she thought. *What I* don't want *is to study French verbs.*

It was Monday evening, and Elizabeth was hunched over her desk, trying to memorize the conjugations of irregular verbs for the French quiz in Ms. Dalton's class the next day. She'd been trying to study for an hour, but she couldn't concentrate. As soon as she tried to go over a verb in her head, she found herself repeating Todd's name, or Jessica's.

Elizabeth rubbed her weary eyes and made another stab at it. "*Je peux, tu peux, il/elle peut*," she read. "I can, you can, he/she can. *Je peux, tu peux, il/elle peut, je peux . . . Non, je ne peux pas!*" she said finally, slamming the book shut.

It was time to talk to Jessica, Elizabeth realized. Until Elizabeth explained the situation to her, she wasn't going to have any peace. When Elizabeth and Ken had driven over to Todd's that fateful night the week before, Jessica hadn't given Elizabeth a chance to tell her side of the story. And since then Jessica had refused to speak to her—unless she had something particularly nasty to say. Elizabeth couldn't really blame her. Jessica thought Elizabeth had been trying to steal her boyfriend away from her. Somehow Elizabeth had to let her know that that wasn't the case.

Well, decided Elizabeth, just because Jessica

wasn't speaking to her didn't mean she couldn't speak to Jessica.

Elizabeth stood up with determination and swiftly crossed the bathroom adjoining the twins' rooms. Usually Jessica's door was wide open, but now it was shut.

Elizabeth tapped on the door softly. There was no response. Elizabeth knocked again. No answer.

Elizabeth pushed the door open and peeked in. Jessica was sitting cross-legged on the floor in the middle of what looked like an avalanche, scribbling something on a piece of paper.

"Don't you knock?" Jessica asked, repeating Elizabeth's favorite line.

"I did knock," Elizabeth said.

"Well, there's nobody here," said Jessica, scooting her legs around and turning her back on Elizabeth.

"What are you doing?" Elizabeth asked, venturing into the room. "Are you writing a cheer?"

"What I'm doing is not speaking to you," said Jessica childishly.

"Fine." Elizabeth sighed. "You don't have to say anything. But could you just listen for a few minutes?"

"I'll give you five minutes," Jessica said, flipping around and leaning against the bed, her arms folded squarely across her chest.

Elizabeth began pacing through the piles of clothing strewn about on the floor. "I want to explain about the other night," she began. "I know it looked bad, but it isn't as bad as you think. When

31

you started dating Ken, I still had unresolved feelings for him. And I didn't feel happy for you, because I was jealous."

Elizabeth stopped and sat on the bed, waiting to see if Jessica would respond. Jessica just sat on the floor in silence, her eyes fixed on the bureau across the room. Elizabeth took a deep breath and plunged ahead. "So I pretended I was you so I could find out how I felt. And what I found out is that I felt nothing. And I want you to know that it was all my fault. Ken didn't know anything about it. He kissed me because he thought I was you. And he stopped as soon as he realized I wasn't."

Elizabeth slid off the bed and knelt down by Jessica, looking at her imploringly. "Jessica, you have to believe me. I wasn't trying to steal your boyfriend. I was just trying to seal off the past. So I could get over Ken. And so I could be happy for you."

Jessica stood up suddenly. "I don't want to hear another word of this," she said angrily, throwing her pen and pad on the bed. "I don't care what your intentions were. What if you had found out that you still had feelings for Ken, Liz?" Jessica kicked at the clothing on the floor. "Then what would you have done? Sneaked around again like you did when Todd was gone?" Jessica looked away in disgust. "You and Ken make me sick, with all your sneaking around. You two are meant for each other."

"But . . . but we're not sneaking around," Elizabeth protested.

32

Jessica ignored her. "And you know what else, Liz?" she sneered. "I don't believe you. I think you still have feelings for Ken. You couldn't stand to see me and Ken together, so you forced us to break up. And now you want me to be your friend again. Well, Liz, you can't have your cake and eat it too."

Tears began to trickle down Elizabeth's face as Jessica continued her diatribe.

"Look, Liz," Jessica spat out finally. "Why don't you just admit the truth? You wanted to get me back for blackmailing you, so you decided to steal my boyfriend." She fixed her sister with a piercing look. "Well, you won, Liz. Are you happy now?"

Elizabeth stared at her sister in shock, amazed that she didn't believe her. Her shock quickly turned to hurt as Elizabeth mentally replayed the angry accusations Jessica had thrown at her. But her hurt rapidly transformed into anger. Jessica had no right to act so high-and-mighty. She hadn't exactly been acting like an angel lately, thought Elizabeth self-righteously. Elizabeth had forgiven Jessica for blackmailing her. Not only had she forgiven her, but she had actually helped her out when she'd had trouble with the squad.

Well, decided Elizabeth stubbornly, she had made her effort. She wasn't going to beg for Jessica's forgiveness any longer. She was sick and tired of being a sap when it came to her sister. If Jessica wanted a fight, then she would get it.

"Well, if you don't believe me," Elizabeth said, standing up and speaking in a cold, removed tone, "then that's your business."

"I don't. Now, would you mind leaving?" Jessica asked. "Because your five minutes are up, and I'm not speaking to you any longer!"

"Well, that's fine with me," retorted Elizabeth. "Because I'm not speaking to you, either!" With that, she stormed out of the room, slamming the door behind her.

Chapter 3

"OK, guys, let's get psyched!" Jessica said on Tuesday afternoon at practice. "We've got three days to get in shape for nationals. We looked great at State, and we're going to look even better in Yosemite."

Jessica was determined to get the squad back on track. She and Heather had called for double practices all week, and the practice session that morning had been disastrous. The girls had wasted the entire morning trying to imitate Heather's combination jump—at Heather's suggestion, of course. Heather knew perfectly well that the other girls wouldn't be able to do it. It was just another opportunity for her to show off. But Jessica was determined not to waste any more time. She wasn't going to let Heather undermine her authority any further.

"So," continued Jessica, "Heather and I have come up with a schedule of our best routines for nationals. We'll start out with the combination we did at state. Now, everybody get in position for the 'Funky Monkey.'"

Jessica took her place in front as all the girls lined up behind her.

"C'mon everybody, do the 'Fun-ky Monkey'!" sang out Jessica, taking two steps to the right and turning in a circle.

"S-V-H's a-rockin', we're groovin' and we're hunky!" she called out.

All the girls joined in as Jessica led them through a series of intricate moves. "We're SVH, we're SVH," the girls called out, clapping their hands and hitting their thighs, "and we're funkin'.'"

"Fun-ky, fun-ky," chanted Jade Wu and Patty Gilbert, snapping their fingers on the sidelines.

"The Funky Monkey," finished the girls, shooting up in the air in stag leaps and coming down in unison in landing splits.

"Funky, funky!" said Jade and Patty again, putting on dark sunglasses and pointing at an imaginary audience.

The girls burst into laughter and collapsed onto the ground, repeating "funky, funky" and cocking their hands at the stands.

"Great, you guys!" exclaimed Jessica. "Now let's try it from the top one more time. This time I'll face you."

The girls got in line and Jessica assumed her position in front of them. "C'mon, everybody—" Suddenly Jessica stopped as she realized that Heather was sitting on the sidelines.

36

"Is there a problem?" asked Jessica, her voice flat.

"Oh, no, no problem," said Heather sweetly. "I thought I'd just sit out the warm-up."

"Here we go again," Lila sighed under her breath, sliding down to lean against the bench.

"The festivities begin," said Amy, joining Lila on the ground. She pulled off her ponytail holder and shook out her long blond hair.

Jessica shot them a warning look and fixed Heather with a steely stare. "This isn't a warm-up," said Jessica.

"Well, if you want to go ahead and repeat all our old cheers at nationals, that's fine with me," said Heather. "But I really don't think it's necessary for me to go through all of them again."

"Heather, as I recall," said Jessica through clenched teeth, "we decided *together* to perform these cheers at nationals."

"Oh, well, we must have just had a slight mis-understanding. I thought we were just choosing our best cheers. I never *dreamed* you'd want to re-peat our old cheers for the national competition," said Heather, her tone sugar sweet.

"And I suppose you have a better suggestion," said Jessica, her voice strained.

"Obviously, if we want to win at nationals, we have to come up with an entirely new set of cheers," said Heather in a haughty tone.

"Which *you* just happen to have made up al-ready," said Jessica.

"Well, I did come up with a few new routines

this weekend," said Heather. She flashed the girls an enthusiastic smile. "I'd love to show them to you. They're jazzy combinations, but technically complicated as well. If we could get them down, I think we'd really knock them dead at nationals."

"Heather, we have got exactly three days to prepare for the national competition. Three days," said Jessica, her voice strong. "We can either spend this time wisely perfecting our old cheers or waste it trying to learn brand-new ones. Perfection or mediocrity—it's your choice." Jessica faced Heather head-on, an unspoken challenge in her eyes.

"You're right, Jessica," said Heather sweetly. "We shouldn't take the chance. After all, better be safe than sorry, right? And we'll probably end up in the top ten anyway."

"I want to learn Heather's new cheers!" interjected Annie.

"Yeah," chimed in Jeanie. "Our routine's getting kind of old."

"I think Jessica's right," put in Lila, trying to help Jessica out. "It would be suicide to try to learn new cheers now."

"Well, why don't we take a vote?" suggested Elizabeth. *Always the diplomat*, thought Jessica, annoyed.

"OK, all in favor of learning new cheers, raise your hands," said Elizabeth. Jessica grimaced as half the squad raised their hands. "All in favor of doing our old cheers, raise your hands." Jessica held her breath as the rest of the girls raised their hands. It was a tie. Jessica threw up her hands in frustration. It was clearly impossible to get anything done with Heather around.

"Well, why don't we do half and half?" suggested Maria. "Half of our old cheers and half of our new cheers."

"That's fine with me," said Heather cheerfully. "But we have to make sure Jessica agrees. After all, she's the other captain."

Jessica was fuming. Now they were going to spend the entire week learning Heather's new cheers. And if she didn't agree to the idea, she would look like a spoilsport. "Sure, no problem," said Jessica shortly, her jaw clenched.

"Great!" said Heather, jumping up. "Now, first, I want to show you the 'Mambo Jamba.' It's a pretty sexy cheer, with a Latino influence."

Jessica gritted her teeth and got into line with the rest of the girls. She couldn't believe it. Heather had done it again.

Elizabeth flipped her gym bag over her shoulder and hurried out of the gym. Practice was finally over. She didn't know how much more of this cheerleading charade she could take. Not only were she and Jessica not speaking, but the cat fight between Heather and Jessica was getting unbearable.

Suddenly Elizabeth stopped dead in her tracks. Todd was coming her way from the opposite end of the football field on his way out of basketball practice. Elizabeth's heart started pounding in her chest. Todd looked so handsome in his blue sweats and white T-shirt. His strong, athletic frame was outlined by his clothes, and his dark-brown hair was ruffled from the wind.

Elizabeth instinctively turned back to the gym, but then she caught herself. This was the first time she'd seen Todd alone since they'd broken up. Because he'd refused to give her a chance to explain, she'd been too upset to pursue him. But he did deserve an explanation. She didn't blame him for being hurt. Elizabeth hesitated. She didn't have much of an explanation to give him. What if he wouldn't forgive her? Well, she decided, she could at least give it a try. She wasn't about to give him up without a fight.

"Todd!" called Elizabeth, hurrying up to him.

"Hi, Elizabeth," Todd said, his voice cold. He walked past her without even turning his head.

"Todd, please!" Elizabeth implored. "Just hear me out for a minute."

Todd turned and stopped, his arms folded across his chest.

Elizabeth stared at him. Now that she finally had his attention, she found herself at a loss for words. Todd took a step as if to walk off. "Wait!" Elizabeth said, catching his arm. Todd flinched and pulled away from her. Elizabeth, hurt, forged ahead anyway.

"I—I just want to apologize for seeing Ken while you were away in Vermont—and for not telling you about it," Elizabeth began. "I know how wrong it was, and I know how much I've hurt you. And I want to try to explain. . . ." Elizabeth hesitated and swallowed hard. "Todd, after you moved to Vermont, I had no intention of seeing Ken. I don't know how it happened. I guess we both missed you, and we turned to each other in your absence. But it didn't mean anything. And we should have told you about it right away when you came back. But I felt so confused and so guilty—" Tears came to Elizabeth's eyes. She'd always prided herself on her honesty. She glanced at Todd through her tears, but he looked unmoved, staring at her with unfathomable eyes.

"And then, when Jessica started seeing him, I felt—I felt confused again. Because I'd never really resolved my feelings for Ken." Elizabeth could see Todd visibly wince, and she took a deep breath. "So I went out with him just to see, to find out if there were feelings between us. And, Todd, I know it sounds horrible, but I wanted to be fair. I wanted to be fair to you and to us. I needed to know once and for all. Does that make any sense to you?" She looked up at him with pleading eyes, but his expression remained inscrutable.

"So, uh, when we were out on that date, we kissed," Elizabeth continued. "And there was nothing there. I realized then and there that the only person I wanted to be with was you. And now I'm afraid I've lost you forever. Todd, I'm so sorry about what I've done. I'll never cheat on you again. You're the one I love."

Elizabeth stopped and looked up at him, feeling completely vulnerable.

✦　　✦　　✦

Todd was incredulous as he listened to Elizabeth ramble on. Did she think she could just say she was sorry and everything would be better? What kind of a fool did she think he was?

Todd had been deeply wounded, and his pride had taken a serious bruising. He had forgiven Elizabeth when she'd had a fling with Luke the summer she was in London. Of course, he'd had a little fling of his own. But this was different. She fooled around with his best friend! Behind his back!

He'd trusted them, Todd berated himself. To think he'd asked Ken to look after Elizabeth. *He sure did a good job looking after her,* Todd thought bitterly. And then they went out *again* when he was around! Well, Todd was sick of playing Mr. Nice Guy. Elizabeth couldn't get Ken, so now she wanted Todd back. But Todd wasn't going to play second fiddle to anybody, *especially* not to his best friend.

And now she was giving him this story about her date with Ken. That she didn't have any feelings for Ken. That she had been thinking about Todd the whole time. Well, maybe he had trusted her once, but he wasn't going to make the same mistake twice.

"Look, Elizabeth," said Todd finally, his voice even. "You can save your breath. You're not the person I thought you were, and I'm better off without you."

Elizabeth stared at him, openmouthed.

"Hope Ken likes your latest cheer," Todd bit out as he left.

Elizabeth watched him go, tears trickling down her cheeks. *I've lost the only boy I could ever really love,* she thought. *And it's all my fault.*

"The salsa routine?" said Heather on Thursday afternoon at practice, an incredulous look on her face. "For the grand finale? You've got to be kidding."

Jessica fought to keep her temper in check. She had come up with the funky salsa cheer by herself. It was the routine that her squad had presented at the cheer-off, the competition between Jessica's and Heather's squads to see which team would go to regionals. The students had loved it. And Mr. Jenkins, the ACA representative, had been so impressed with it that he had recommended combining the two squads for the regional competition.

"I suppose you'd rather do a cheer of your own," said Jessica. "For the sake of the team, of course."

"Well, I certainly don't care whose idea it is," said Heather with a small flip of her head. "It's just that the salsa routine is lacking a little *je ne sais quoi,* if you know what I mean."

"No, I'm afraid I don't," said Jessica flatly. "Care to translate, Mademoiselle Mallone?"

"Well, to be perfectly blunt, it's not jazzy enough," said Heather. "I mean, it's completely adequate. But it's not going to make the judges notice us. If we want to win at nationals, we've got to stand out. We've got to do something really special."

"Like one of your new cheers, for example?" Jessica said, her voice dripping with sarcasm.

"For example," said Heather, pretending not to notice Jessica's tone. "I was hoping we could do the new hip-hop routine I've been working on. It's sure to bring the house down."

"Cool!" exclaimed Jade Wu. "We could add some neat dance steps."

"Yeah," said Annie, "it'll be like a rap video."

"MTV, here we come," said Sandy, drawing a general laugh.

Jessica didn't bother putting it up for a vote. She knew what the girls would say. Heather had them so bamboozled that they would do anything she said. They thought she had the magic recipe for winning the national competition.

"Sure, great idea," said Jessica, thinking quickly. Before practice she had resolved not to let Heather take over, and she was still determined to meet that goal. "But before we start practice, I think we should decide on the uniforms we're going to wear for the grand finale."

The girls gathered around on the field while Jessica pulled out the sample uniforms she had ordered from Cheer Ahead, the sporting-clothes outfitter. They were standard red-and-white cheerleading outfits with a twist: matching full-body unitards. Jessica held them up for everyone to see. "Classic, beautiful, right?" said Jessica. "But look," she said, indicating the red Lycra unitards. "Catsuits for an added touch."

"They're fabulous!" said Lila.

44

"The catsuits are great!" breathed Amy. "We'll look so sharp when we're flipping."

"They're the latest," said Jessica, smiling with satisfaction. She handed the uniforms around for the girls to examine. They were met with approval by everybody.

When the uniform came around to Heather, she held it up in the air and wrinkled her nose delicately.

"What's wrong, Heather?" Jessica sneered. "Are the uniforms offending your senses?"

"No, of course not," replied Heather. "They're just a little, ah, traditional. It's just a little surprising, coming from you. You're usually so, um, faddy."

Jessica could feel her face burning. Not only was Heather insulting her uniforms, she was insulting her style as well. "Yeah, well, I always thought it was better to be faddy than cheap," said Jessica angrily.

"OK, you two," said Amy, holding up a hand. "Heather, why don't you show us your uniforms, and we'll decide together?"

"Well, I had these custom-made," said Heather, holding up a sample uniform. Jessica couldn't believe it. The uniforms consisted of tiny Lycra half tops and red-and-white-checked miniskirts that fell at the hip. Jessica couldn't imagine how they could possibly walk in them, let alone cheer in them.

"They're perfect," Annie Whitman breathed. "Hipsters for our hip-hop cheer!"

"They're great," agreed Maria. "We'll be the hippest squad around."

Elizabeth, as usual, put it to a vote. Jessica seethed as she watched the majority of hands go up in favor of Heather's uniforms. Only Lila, Amy, and Elizabeth stood by her.

"Oh, well, I really think we should use the cute little uniforms Jessica chose," Heather said after the votes had been cast. "After all, Jessica is the co-captain. And she went to so much trouble."

"Don't even consider it," said Jessica shortly. "Now, if you'll excuse me," she said, getting up abruptly, "I don't think I'm really necessary with hippy, hip-hop Heather around." Jessica turned and stalked off without looking back.

"Jessica! Wait!" came a male voice from across the field.

Jessica looked across the football field. It was Ken Matthews on his way from football practice. He was wearing a cutoff T-shirt over his shoulder pads and carrying a football helmet. Jessica turned her head and continued to stomp across the field, but her heart started pounding in spite of herself. Ken looked stronger and handsomer than ever in his football gear.

"Jessica!" Ken yelled again, running after her. "I want to talk to you!"

Well, I don't want to talk to you, thought Jessica stubbornly. Ken Matthews was a waste of her time. If he couldn't distinguish her from Elizabeth, then he obviously didn't feel anything for her in particular; he just liked her type.

Ken caught up to her and ran in front of her, blocking her path. Jessica stopped and faced him, her eyes a stony blue. "If you're looking for Elizabeth," she said in an icy tone, "she's still at practice." She turned on her heel and walked away.

Chapter 4

"On behalf of the entire school, I want to thank all the girls on the cheerleading squad for their continued support of our athletic teams," said Mr. Cooper, the principal, his loud voice booming across the auditorium.

Jessica fidgeted in her seat, anxious to get on the road. The weekend of the national competition had arrived, and the entire school was sending the team off in royal style. The school had organized a huge pep rally in the auditorium, to be followed by a parade out to the parking lot with the marching band playing. The auditorium was a festive sight. The walls were adorned with banners and pennants, and multicolored streamers and balloons hung from the bleachers.

"The cheerleading squad is the power behind the throne, the strength behind the success of our teams . . ." said Mr. Cooper.

Jessica yawned and leaned over to Lila. "Isn't he overdoing it a bit?" she whispered.

Lila rolled her eyes. "Yeah, old Chrome Dome's in fine form this morning," she said.

". . . behind the football team, the basketball team, the soccer team, and the track team," continued the principal. As he mentioned each sport, the teams stood up in blocks, yelling and hooting. "And they're a strength in and of themselves," finished Mr. Cooper. "For the first time in the history of Sweet Valley High, the girls' cheerleading squad has won the state competition. And for the first time in the history of our school, the cheerleading squad is competing in the national competition!"

The auditorium filled with the sounds of students hooting and cheering. "Way to go, cheerleaders!" "SVH all the way!" Streamers and confetti were thrown into the air, and the band broke into a rousing version of the school song.

After the band had finished, Mr. Cooper held up a hand for the audience to settle down. "And now I'd like to turn the mike over to Ken Matthews, the captain of the football team and Sweet Valley's star quarterback."

Whistles and catcalls accompanied Ken's trip across the auditorium.

"Please, cash contributions only," he said, grinning as he took the mike. The audience laughed and Ken paused, his face turning serious. He cleared his throat and spoke into the microphone. "This year we had an outstanding season. We won the divisional and regional championships, and

49

more important, we beat the Big Mesa Bulls, our greatest rivals."

Ken paused while cheers filled the air. "And I just want to say, we couldn't have done it without the cheerleaders' support. We'd have been nothing without Jessica Wakefield and her squad cheering us on—behind us all the way through thick and thin."

Jessica's face flushed as Ken spoke. She felt as if he were speaking directly to her. She stole a glance in Heather's direction to see if she'd noticed she hadn't been mentioned. Heather was staring straight ahead, a pout marring her delicate features. She'd flirted with Ken the entire time Jessica was seeing him, but Ken hadn't paid any attention to her. Jessica felt a surge of satisfaction and turned her attention back to the floor.

"So to the entire cheerleading squad," Ken finished, "these are from all of us to all of you." Ken laid a bunch of red roses on the podium and walked off the stage.

The crowd roared. "Speech! Speech! Speech!" demanded the students.

Before Jessica could react, Heather was on her feet and racing across the auditorium. When she reached the podium, she gathered the roses under her arm and picked up the microphone. "On behalf of my squad, I'd like to thank you all for your tremendous support. . . ."

"It's unbelievable," Jessica said to Lila. "That girl's a real piece of work."

"She really is revolting," Lila agreed.

"This is too much," said Amy, leaning over. "Those roses were meant for you. Heather steals the show every time."

"Well, not this time," said Jessica resolutely, jumping out of her seat. Heather might have stolen the limelight at State, but Jessica wasn't going to sit on the sidelines this time, not in her own school. She quickly ran across the stage and joined Heather at the podium. Heather stared at her openmouthed as Jessica grabbed the mike.

"Sweet Valley High's cheerleading squad is the greatest in the entire state of California!" Jessica yelled. "And we're going to be the greatest in the nation. We're going to get out there and win this weekend—for our teams and for our school!"

The crowd roared its approval, rising to its feet and yelling. Jessica picked up the mike again and called the squad to the field. The girls ran onto the stage and gave an impressive performance of their new hip-hop routine. The crowd ate it up, tapping their feet and chanting to the music.

At the end of the routine Heather finished with an unexpected jump, a spectacular series of one-armed cartwheels followed by a no-hands back flip. Undaunted, Jessica followed with a dazzling jump of her own, a trojan-jump combination ending with a landing in the splits.

"Is this for real?" Lila said to Amy.

Amy rolled her eyes. "Just another episode of the Jessica-Heather show."

"Tune in tomorrow," Lila said with a sigh.

❖ ❖ ❖

"Wow, that was quite a pep rally!" exclaimed Enid Rollins, Elizabeth's best friend, as she accompanied her to the parking lot.

"It really was, wasn't it?" said Elizabeth, her cheeks glowing. The excitement was intoxicating, and Elizabeth found herself swept up in it. The entire student body was accompanying the cheerleaders to the parking lot, and the energy in the crowd was palpable. The students had formed a parade, throwing streamers and cheering as they poured out of the building. The band was heading up the rear, playing a medley of victory songs.

"Is that the bus?" Enid gasped as they arrived at the vehicle designated to transport the cheerleaders to Yosemite.

"Pretty impressive, huh?" Elizabeth laughed. The cheerleaders had spent hours decorating the bus the night before. They had covered it in psychedelic colors and wild abstract designs. A banner streamed off the back, with the words SWEET VALLEY RULES! written in bold purple block letters.

"Well, have a great time!" Enid said. "It looks like this won't be as bad as you thought."

"Thanks, Enid!" said Elizabeth. "I'll call you first thing when we get back." She mounted the steps and waved cheerfully as Enid walked away.

Suddenly Elizabeth caught sight of Todd standing alone on the sidewalk. He cut a lonely figure, looking lost and forlorn at the far end of the parking lot. The pain of losing him washed over Elizabeth again, and she fought down a feeling of physical nausea. The horrible, judgmental words that Todd had thrown at her came back again, echoing in her head. *You're not the person I thought you were, you're not the person I thought you were.* Elizabeth shook her head hard, trying to rid it of the painful thoughts. She wrenched her eyes away from Todd and headed into the bus. "SVH is number one! SVH is number one!" chanted a group of football players as they carried Jessica across the parking lot on their shoulders. Jessica beamed and she blew kisses to the crowd, basking in the glory of the moment.

As they reached the bus, Tim Nelson and Scott Trost deposited Jessica gently on the asphalt. Jessica hopped down and climbed up the steps, turning to wave at the crowd. The students whistled and cheered, yelling "Good luck!" and "Knock 'em dead, Jessica!"

Jessica mounted the steps and climbed into the front seat, feeling like a queen. She looked out the window and caught a glimpse of Ken Matthews staring longingly after the bus. Jessica felt a stab of regret as she remembered Ken's effort to talk to her earlier in the week. But she quickly banished the thought from her mind. *He's probably pining for Elizabeth. Well, I'll never speak to him ever again,* she vowed, blowing kisses at all her fans through the window.

As the bus pulled away, Todd kicked at the gravel in the parking lot, wondering for the thousandth time how his life had gotten so bad so fast.

One day he thought he was the luckiest guy in the world, with the best girlfriend and the greatest best friend—and the next day he lost them both, to each other!

Once again the images of Ken and Elizabeth came to his mind, tormenting him. He pictured them together while he'd been alone in Vermont—running on the beach, stopping for an intimate talk, kissing each other passionately. . . . Todd shook his head hard, forcing his thoughts in a different direction. He had to stop torturing himself like this.

Elizabeth looked so sad getting on the bus, thought Todd. And so beautiful. He knew she must be miserable going to nationals with the cheerleading squad. He wondered how Jessica had roped her into that one. He wished he had forgiven her, so he could have seen her off—and held her for a moment before she left. *But you were stubborn as usual,* Todd berated himself. Elizabeth had asked for his forgiveness and he'd refused. And now it was too late. She was leaving, and she wouldn't have anything to do with him. Feeling sorry for himself, Todd plodded back into the school building.

At the same time, Ken Matthews was slowly making his way toward the door of Sweet Valley High, lost in thoughts of his own. Jessica had created quite a stir at the pep rally. Her final jump had brought down the house. Jessica made cheerleading seem like an art, thought Ken with admiration. She was talented and beautiful—and feisty. Nobody pushed Jessica Wakefield around. *That's probably why I like her so much,* thought Ken. *She's strong and sexy—and I've let her slip through my fingers.*

Ken had tried to send Jessica a private message through his public speech, but she hadn't so much as glanced at him. *If only I'd told Todd about Elizabeth from the beginning, none of this would have happened,* Ken chided himself. *Todd and I would still be friends, Todd and Elizabeth would still be together, and Jessica . . . Jessica would still be mine.*

As Todd got up to the door, the crowd piling into the school bottlenecked. He felt somebody shoving him against the door. Todd turned and found himself face-to-face with Ken Matthews. Anger boiled up inside him as he confronted his back-stabbing friend.

"Hey, man, get off of me!" yelled Todd, placing his hands squarely on Ken's chest and shoving him away.

"I didn't touch you!" Ken shouted back. He pushed him back with all his might, sending Todd reeling against the brick wall of the school building. Students jumped out of their way, and the crowd formed a circle around them.

Todd's eyes bulged with rage. "Keep your hands to yourself!" he yelled. "Leave me and my girlfriend alone!" He hurtled forward and aimed his fist at Ken's face.

Ken warded off the blow. "It's not my fault if you can't keep a girlfriend!" shouted Ken, directing a blow at Todd's stomach. "Maybe you should blame Elizabeth and not me!" Todd jumped adeptly to the side and hopped back and forth as he faced his adversary, a savage look on his face.

The crowd around them began to chant. "Fight! Fight! Fight!"

"The Wakefield girls aren't worth all this trouble!" taunted Bruce Patman from the crowd.

Ken and Todd looked up simultaneously and charged at Bruce like enraged bulls, jumping on him and wrestling him to the ground.

"All right! All right! Break it up!" yelled Mr. Collins, arriving on the scene. He tried to pull the boys off Bruce, but the two of them were oblivious, rolling around on the ground as they tried to get Bruce locked in a pin. Tim Nelson and Robbie Hendricks went for Todd, while Tad Johnson and Scott Trost turned to Ken. Finally the four of them managed to wrench the boys away from Bruce.

As the football players held Todd and Ken back, Bruce stood up insolently and wiped the dirt off his jeans. "Girls got you a little worked up, huh?" Bruce said, a jeering challenge in his eyes.

"Lemme at him!" growled Todd, struggling with his captors. Ken swiped at the air in vain while Tad and Scott held him back.

"I'm afraid you two need to have a chat with the principal," Mr. Collins said, putting his hands on their shoulders. Todd and Ken stopped struggling, and the boys dropped their hold. "Follow me, please," said Mr. Collins, escorting them to Mr. Cooper's office. The boys followed him begrudgingly, both sullen and not speaking. Bruce snickered as they were led away.

"I do not tolerate fighting in my school," said Mr. Cooper, looking like a puffed-up bird sitting behind his solid-oak desk. "Sweet Valley High prides itself on offering the finest education and the highest-quality moral training. Here at Sweet Valley all the students adhere to a strict code of ethics. *All the students,*" Mr. Cooper repeated. "Is that clear?"

"Yes, sir," said Todd and Ken together, listening politely as the principal went on. "A gentleman settles his arguments with words, not weapons," boomed Mr. Cooper, raising a forefinger into the air. "The lash of the tongue is mightier than the thrust of the sword."

Todd and Ken nodded solemnly. Todd bit his lip and stared at the floor to prevent himself from smiling. Chrome Dome Cooper was famous for his stuffiness, and now he was outdoing himself. "The penalty for causing a ruckus in this school is not light, not light indeed. Now, do you know what that penalty is?" asked Mr. Cooper, fixing them both with a menacing stare. Todd and Ken shook their heads.

"Expulsion—*that* is the penalty for fighting in school," said Mr. Cooper. He slapped his hand on his desk for emphasis and stood up.

Both Todd and Ken hung their heads. *I wish he'd get to the point,* thought Todd.

"Now," said Mr. Cooper, dragging out his words and pacing around the office, "because you two both have outstanding records, I'm going to let you off easy this time. Just this one time, you understand?" He paused, cocking an eyebrow and looking in their direction. "I'm giving you both detention for the entire week."

"Yes, sir," Todd and Ken mumbled together.

"That's it. You're dismissed," said Mr. Cooper, sitting down again behind his desk and folding his hands underneath his double chin. "Run along now."

"Thank you, sir," said the boys, nodding deferentially as they stood up and walked out of the office.

"And don't let me hear anything about your fighting again!" Todd could hear Mr. Cooper call out after them.

Todd and Ken walked silently down the hallway.

"A real gentleman settles his arguments with words, not weapons," said Ken as soon as they had safely turned the corner, imitating Mr. Cooper's deep, grave voice.

Todd stuck a finger in the air. "The lash of the tongue is mightier than the thrust of the sword!" he exclaimed.

"Now, you boys have created quite a ruckus!" Ken went on in a booming voice.

"For which the punishment is very grave," continued Todd.

"Ten years in the federal penitentiary!" said Ken.

"To be followed by the death penalty!" added Todd. The two boys broke out into gales of laughter. Ken held up an open palm and Todd slapped him a high five.

Suddenly Ken dropped his hand and stood still. Todd stopped walking as he did, and an awkward silence filled the air.

Ken cleared his throat and looked serious. "Hey, man," he said, "I'm really sorry about what happened with Elizabeth. It was a mistake, and it didn't mean anything. We should have told you about it right away." Ken paused, and a pained look crossed his face. "I really messed everything up," he said. "Your relationship with Elizabeth, my relationship with Jessica—and our friendship."

"Well, you did mess things up a bit, but that's all in the past now," said Todd. "Apology accepted." He stuck out his hand for Ken to shake. "Let's call a truce."

Ken heaved a sigh of relief and clasped Todd's hand in his. He felt as if a huge burden had been lifted from him.

"But from now on, don't forget which twin is yours," Todd warned teasingly as they resumed walking down the hall.

"Don't worry about it. It'll never happen again," said Ken. "In fact, this is only solving half the problem. Now we've got to get you and Elizabeth back together."

"And although I'll never understand the attraction," replied Todd, "you and Jessica were obviously meant for each other."

"But there's not a lot we can do now with the girls all the way in Yosemite at nationals," said Ken.

"Hmm," Todd pondered. "Of course, we do have a three-day weekend."

Suddenly both of them stopped and looked at each other.

"Road trip?" said Ken, noting the glint in Todd's eye. "We'll take my car," said Todd, nodding. "I'll pick you up at four o'clock."

Chapter 5

"Wow, this is beautiful," Jessica said as the bus pulled through the gates of the national-cheerleading compound in Yosemite. The grounds were lush and sprawling, covered with huge redwood trees and luxurious flower beds.

"Like entering paradise," Lila said dryly. She rubbed her neck and stretched her arms above her head. "I thought we'd never get here." The bus ride had taken about six hours, and they hadn't made a single pit stop.

"Cheerleading paradise, in any case," said Amy, twisting around to face Jessica and Lila. "Have you ever seen so many cheerleaders in one place?"

"It's enough to make one sick," Lila said, propping her knees against the seat in front of her with an exaggerated sigh.

"Lila, *you're* enough to make one sick," said Jessica, elbowing her friend teasingly. "Now, get in the spirit of things," she commanded.

"Aye, aye, cocaptain," said Lila, giving Jessica a salute. She raised her arms above her head in a V formation, mocking their Victory cheer.

"Lila, you're hopeless," Jessica said, throwing up her hands and gazing out the window.

Jessica sucked in her breath as the bus weaved its way through the rolling hills of the cheerleading compound. "We're in the big league now," she said, taking in the landscape. The grounds were practically swarming with cheerleaders, each one seemingly more talented than the next. Squads from all over the country were practicing their routines with aplomb, jumping and flipping like pros.

"We really are," agreed Amy, her voice sounding awed. "Nobody's even noticed us."

"Or our wildly decorated bus," added Lila.

"Somehow I expected to make a splash when we arrived," mused Jessica. "We were sent off like celebrities when we left, and here we're invisible."

Suddenly things stood out in clear perspective for Jessica. In Sweet Valley they ruled. Now they were just one of the many teams from all over the country competing for the title of best cheerleading squad. Jessica pondered the gravity of it all. If they won, they would be the best cheerleaders in the entire country. Wouldn't that, in essence, make her the best cheerleader in the country— since she'd be the captain of the best team in the country?

"OK! Everybody up! Let's go!" Jessica's reverie was rudely interrupted by the grating sound of

Heather's irritating voice. Jessica's visions of glory came to a grinding halt as she remembered that she wasn't the captain of the cheerleading squad, but the cocaptain. Not only that, but Heather · bane-of-Jessica's-existence was the other cocaptain. As long as she was cocaptain, she'd never be the best cheerleader in the country, thought Jessica, annoyed.

"Unload the bags first!" yelled Heather from up front, barking out orders like a drill sergeant. "Pom-pom bags, uniforms, hand 'em up!" Jessica's eyes narrowed as she watched Heather brazenly take charge. The girls obeyed her like a flock of sheep. Making a conveyor-belt formation, the girls stood up in the aisle and smoothly handed the supplies down the line. Heather took the bags as they were passed forward and threw them onto the lawn.

"OK, everybody off!" yelled Heather as soon as all the equipment was unloaded. She hopped out of the bus and stood by the door, shooing the cheerleaders out.

"She could use a whistle," whispered Lila to Jessica as they made their way down the aisle with the rest of the girls.

"Do you think she's going to strip-search us?" whispered Jessica back.

"Move it on out!" yelled Heather as Jessica and Lila approached the stairs. Jessica stopped and put her hand on the banister, fixing Heather with a steely stare. Their eyes met for one long moment, an unspoken challenge hanging in the air. Jessica's face set in determination. This was the most important event in her life, and she wasn't going to let Heather Mallone ruin it for her. She wasn't going to let her take over. More than ever she wanted to win, and more than ever she wished that bossy Heather Mallone had never shown her face at Sweet Valley High.

"Heather, I think we're all capable of getting off the bus by ourselves," said Jessica calmly. Deliberately moving at a maddeningly slow pace, she walked gracefully down the two big steps. She paused on the bottom step to wipe some imaginary dirt off her shoe. The she stood up and smiled at Heather as she stepped delicately to the ground.

"Here, Jess, why don't you carry these?" said Heather, throwing her an oversize duffel bag full of pom-poms as the girls gathered their supplies to head to their cabin.

Jessica caught the pom-poms in both arms and took a step back, recoiling from the force of the bag. "Heather, do you mind?" she snapped, glaring at her.

Suddenly a tall girl crashed into her, nearly mowing her over. "Hey!" Jessica said, stumbling. She quickly regained her balance and jumped out of the way. The girl just breezed by her, not even bothering to apologize.

Jessica leaned against the bus, the pom-pom bag held to her stomach. *Who's that?* she wondered, staring after the tall, beautiful brunette. With that kind of attitude she'd probably be tough

64

competition. Jessica felt suddenly overwhelmed, like a small fish in a big pond.

"Jessica, are you coming?" yelled Heather. The sound of Heather's strident voice brought Jessica back to reality. Some random, pushy cheerleader was no problem for Jessica. Jessica was confident that she was more talented than all of the cheerleaders there combined. The only person in her way was Heather. And Jessica had to figure out a way to overcome the obstacle.

"We're almost there, guys!" said Elizabeth as she led the girls through the woods to the cabin they were sharing with the squad from Alabama. Jessica and Heather had gone to the main hall to check in, and Heather had put Elizabeth in charge of finding the cabin.

"What's it called? Holly House?" Maria asked, running up beside her.

"Hunter House," said Elizabeth, stopping to peer at the map that laid out the compound. "Shoot!" Elizabeth exclaimed as a breeze came up and whipped through the map, sending small ripples across it. She knelt down and smoothed out the map on the earth, securing it firmly with one knee. Holding her hair back from her face with one hand, Elizabeth examined the map carefully. "I think that's it," she said, pointing in the direction of a rustic log cabin up the hill.

"It's got an *H* on it," confirmed Maria. Elizabeth stood up and brushed off her knees, waving for the group to follow. Elizabeth and

Maria trudged up the hill with the girls close behind, panting from their trek through the woods.

"I wonder if this is part of the competition," said Jeanie breathlessly, leaning on Sandy for support.

"I hope not," responded Sandy, "because I think we'd lose."

"Hunter House," said Maria as they reached the cabin, reading the name printed on a cheerful diamond-shaped yellow sign hanging from the door.

Suddenly a face popped out the door. "Well, hi, y'all!" exclaimed a big freckle-faced southern girl, waving as the Sweet Valley High cheerleaders approached their cabin.

"C'mon in!" said another friendly-looking girl, propping the door of the cabin wide open. "We've been waitin' for you to arrive. Kept wonderin' where the girls from California were! I'm Wilhemina, and this is Peggy May."

"Hi, Wilhemina, I'm Elizabeth," said Elizabeth. She smiled at the superfriendly girl and walked into the airy bungalow.

"You can call me Will," continued the girl, chattering on by Elizabeth's side. "Or Willy, even. Do you go by Liz ever?"

"Sometimes my good friends call me Liz," said Elizabeth, forcing a smile. The girls seemed genuinely friendly, but Elizabeth wasn't in the mood for it. She just wanted to get through this weekend with as little interaction as possible and get home.

"We cleared out half the cabin for you," said a

girl with long blond ponytails high up on her head. "We took the right side," she said, pointing out their belongings. That was obvious, thought Elizabeth as she heaved her duffel bag onto a free bunk. The Alabama girls had already lavishly covered their side of the cabin with Braselton Bulldogs paraphernalia.

"You all psyched for a weekend of stiff competition?" said Wilhemina, hopping up eagerly onto Elizabeth's bunk and crossing her legs comfortably. Elizabeth groaned inwardly. Each one of these girls was more enthusiastic than the next. She couldn't believe she was going to have to spend an entire weekend pretending that she cared about cheerleading.

Elizabeth just nodded and began unpacking her bag. Fortunately, Wilhemina seemed to get the hint and jumped off her bed just as enthusiastically as she had arrived. "Hey, great uniforms!" she said, bounding over to Lila's bunk.

"Aren't they nice?" agreed Lila, holding up a stack of elegant one-piece uniforms. Half of the costumes were solid red and half were solid white. The necks and sleeves were trimmed with lace, and tiny bows ran down the bodice. The costume tapered in at the waist and flared out in a pleated skirt.

"Hey, I haven't seen these before," said Jeanie, running a finger over the soft cotton.

"Yeah, where did these come from?" asked Maria. All the girls gathered around Lila's bunk, picking up the uniforms and admiring them.

67

"I ordered them before we left. It's a surprise," said Lila with a smile. "I thought we could wear these for the grand finale and cool the Jessica-Heather rivalry a bit."

"That's a great idea," said Amy. "We can wear Jessica's uniforms for the salsa routine and Heather's for the hip-hop one."

"I don't think they're going to agree to it," said Elizabeth, coming over to the bunk.

"We'll just tell them it's been decided," said Lila. "Either they go along with it, or else we make them walk the plank." All the girls laughed.

"Sounds like y'all run a tight ship," said Wilhemina with a smile.

"Only when it's necessary," said Maria.

Jeanie stood up and surveyed the room, her hands on her hips. "Looks like you guys have gotten a jump on the decorating," she said to Wilhemina.

"Here, Jeanie, let's put this up," suggested Sandy, holding up a huge Sweet Valley High banner. The girls quickly hung it up, wrapping the string around knots in the wood. The other girls soon got involved, strewing their side of the room with Sweet Valley paraphernalia. They adorned the walls with Gladiator pennants and posters and stuck up red-and-white flags around the bunks. Elizabeth watched in astonishment as their half of the cabin was quickly transformed into a Sweet Valley High fan club.

Elizabeth turned her attention to the task at hand, trying to shut out the sounds of excited chatter. She felt completely divorced from the enthusiastic girls around her. The weekend stretched ahead of her endlessly. She couldn't imagine how she was going to get through this cheerleading extravaganza. She felt completely apathetic, unable even to summon enough energy to help with the decorations.

Giving in to her lassitude, Elizabeth methodically took her clothes out of her duffel bag and placed them in neat piles on the floor. Reaching into her cosmetic bag, she woodenly took out her toiletries one by one and placed them on the little nightstand by her bunk.

When she was done, she shook the bag to see if it was empty. Something clattered inside. Elizabeth fished around in her bag and pulled out the one remaining item. It was a little framed picture of Todd she habitually brought with her on trips. Elizabeth sat down on the bed, gazing at the picture. Todd's handsome face stared back at her, a loving expression in his warm brown eyes. With a sigh Elizabeth placed the picture carefully on the wooden nightstand.

"Hey, is that your boyfriend?" asked Wilhemina, popping up beside her. "He sure is cute!"

"Actually, he's not my boyfriend anymore," said Elizabeth sadly. She picked up the picture from the nightstand and put it back in her duffel bag.

Chapter 6

"Welcome to the Tenth Annual National Cheer-leading Competition in Yosemite!" said the head of the American Cheerleading Association on Friday afternoon at orientation in the auditorium. She was a tall, athletic woman with short-cropped dark-brown hair and an engaging smile. She was dressed in a navy-blue suit, the signature apparel of the directors of the ACA. "I'm Zoe Balsam," she said with a smile. "I may look ancient to you, but I competed here not so long ago. The national competition was the highlight of my high-school career, and I hope it will be the same for you."

Jessica surveyed the crowd around her as the girls clapped. There were fifty squads competing at nationals, fifty squads comprising the most talented cheerleaders in the entire country. Each team was sitting in blocks, decked out in cheer-leading attire representative of their school. Each squad seemed to have its own look, and they all appeared professional and polished. It looked as if they were going to have some serious competition.

"Nationals is a series of seven competitions spread out over three days," announced Ms. Balsam. "The event is broken down into three legs, each of which counts for one third of the total score. You will compete in the first leg on Saturday—a series of three competitions—and the second on Sunday—also a series of three competitions. On Monday is the grand finale, a concluding performance that counts equally for one third of the entire tournament."

Jessica calculated quickly in her head. "That means almost any team can steal on Monday," she said to Amy.

Amy nodded. "It's like the ice-skating program of the Olympics."

"Shh!" Heather said sharply, twisting around from her seat in front of them and giving them a warning look.

Jessica leaned over to Amy again. "It's hard to tell who's the director here," she said in a stage whisper.

Amy covered her mouth, stifling a giggle. Heather turned around and shot Jessica a dirty look.

"Heather, pay attention," said Jessica, pointing to the podium. "Ms. Balsam's speaking."

Heather flounced around in a huff.

"Weekend competitions will be held out in the field, weather permitting," continued Ms. Balsam.

"The grand finale will be held here, in the auditorium. That way the press will have easy access for pictures and interviews of the winning squads."

The press! Jessica thought. She pictured herself splashed across the front page of the *L.A. Times*, a headline reading, "Jessica Wakefield, Best Cheerleader in the Nation." She would give them an exclusive interview, with personal anecdotes and stories highlighting her cheerleading career. Maybe the talk shows would be interested as well, she thought.

"Each competition is worth one hundred points. The teams are judged in four categories: athletic ability, artistic impression, school spirit, and tumbling. Each category is worth twenty-five points," said Ms. Balsam. "And remember," she added, "each competition must include a classic double-herky combination and an original jump. The trojan-crunch combination is mandatory for every team in the final competition."

Jessica whistled under her breath. "Wow, this is complicated," she said to Lila.

Lila shook her head in amazement. "You'd think we were at the Olympics."

"I don't know how we're going to keep track of it," said Jessica.

"Do you mind?" Heather said, whirling around with fire in her eyes. "I am trying to listen."

Jessica rolled her eyes. If Heather continued to act like a den mother all weekend, the competition was going to be unbearable.

"You'll find the guidelines I have discussed so

far all laid out in the guidebook you can pick up on your way out. Dates and times of the competitions are listed as well," finished Ms. Balsam. "Good luck to all of you. I look forward to seeing you tomorrow on the field!"

The Sweet Valley High cheerleaders filed out of the auditorium with the rest of the participants. The entire squad was subdued, a little awed by the magnitude of the event.

"Did you check out the competition?" said Amy to Jessica on the way out of the auditorium. "These girls are hard core!"

Jessica nodded, but her mind wasn't on the competing squads. The only competition she was worried about was Heather.

Todd pulled his shiny black BMW around to the front of Sweet Valley High after school on Friday. His spirits were high. Before evening he would be with Elizabeth again. And he hoped she would forgive him for his bad behavior. He spotted Ken sitting on the bench with some of the football players and let forth two short beeps of the horn. Ken waved good-bye to his friends and jogged up to the car.

"We're in business, man," said Todd, leaning over to open the front door. He revved the engine as Ken folded his long frame into the passenger seat.

"Did you get the info?" asked Ken as Todd pulled out of the lot.

"It's all right here," said Todd, pointing to a tiny

corner of notebook paper sitting on the dashboard. He picked up the paper and waved it in the air with his left hand.

"Nice going, man," said Ken admiringly.

"Yep, everything we need is on these two sheets of paper," said Todd, grabbing the map of the greater-California area off the seat with his free hand. He waved the papers in the air, holding the steering wheel with his elbows.

"Whoa! Both hands on the wheel," said Ken, grabbing the address and map out of Todd's hands. "You drive, I'll direct."

"Yosemite," said Ken out loud, studying the address. "Did you have any problem getting the information?"

"No problem at all," said Todd cheerfully. "I told Mr. Collins I wanted to write to Elizabeth to wish her luck. He was happy to give me the address. He even asked me to send his good wishes as well."

"Brilliant," said Ken, unfolding the map and spreading it out on his lap. He traced his finger along the map, trying to locate the site of the cheerleading competition. "Yosemite is just north of Madera, right?"

Todd nodded. "If we take Route Forty-four, we should be there in about six hours."

"Just in time for a late-night snack with the girls," said Ken, grinning.

"Quick pit stop," said Todd, steering the car adeptly into the parking lot of a convenience store. He pulled up alongside the gas pumps and brought the car to a halt.

"I'll get some supplies," said Ken, jumping out of the car and running into the store. Todd filled up the tank with gas and handed the attendant his credit card. A few minutes later Ken emerged from the building, his arms loaded with a variety of junk food and sodas.

"We're on our way!" said Todd, donning a pair of sunglasses. "Yosemite, here we come!"

"Look out, ladies!" said Ken, giving Todd a high five.

Todd flipped on the radio, fiddling with the knob until he found a station he liked. With the radio blasting Todd turned onto Valley Crest Drive.

"Hey, there's Winston!" said Ken, pointing to the side of the road. Winston Egbert, affectionately known as the class clown, was walking down the sidewalk, balancing a few shopping bags in his arms. He looked even more awkward than usual up to his ears in groceries.

Todd pulled the car to the side of the road and came to a screeching halt by Winston.

"Come on, Egbert," said Todd, "this is the love mobile. We're taking take you to see Maria. Get in." Pretty brown-haired Maria Santelli was Winston's longtime girlfriend.

"What?" said Winston, lowering the groceries and peering out at the boys.

"We're going to the National Cheerleading Competition in Yosemite," explained Todd. "To see Jessica and Elizabeth and Maria—"

"And a couple hundred other girls," added Ken for effect. "C'mon!"

"Sorry, guys, can't," said Winston, shifting from one foot to the other as he juggled the bags in his arms. "I've got a bunch of groceries for my mother."

"Don't worry, she'll understand," Todd insisted. "You can call her when we get there."

"No, I really can't go," said Winston. "I've got to get these groceries home. And then I've got a bunch of chores to do. And there's this old movie on TV that I really want—"

But the boys weren't listening. Todd shut off the ignition and they both jumped out. Todd ran around to the backseat and opened it. "After you," said Ken magnanimously, gesturing to the seat.

"Oh, boy," said Winston, getting in reluctantly. Todd slammed the door after him, and the boys jumped back into the car. Todd put his foot on the gas and sped off toward the desert, tunes blaring.

"I think my mother's ice cream is melting," Winston said from the backseat.

"Got a spoon?" Ken asked.

"It's just all so excitin'!" enthused Wilhemina on Friday night at dinner in the huge cafeteria of the lodge.

"It sure ii-s," said Jessica mischievously, putting on a southern twang. Her blue-green eyes twinkled merrily as she smiled at Wilhemina.

Wilhemina laughed good-naturedly. "You know, Jess," she said, "you and your twin sister Elizabeth may come from California, but with your blond hair and blue eyes, you look like you belong in

76

Alabama! Why, with a little bit of fixin', we could make you two perfect southern belles."

"And we could change you and Peggy May into California beach bums!" said Jessica. She spoke for both herself and Elizabeth, but she didn't bother to look at her sister. "A few days on the beach, a couple of surfing lessons . . ." Jessica grinned, putting her arm around the easygoing girl's shoulder.

The other girls laughed, but Elizabeth just stared down at her plate, playing with her food. The turkey entrée looked good, but she had no appetite. Elizabeth felt completely out of her element. She was sitting at a table with two cheerleading squads in a roomful of hundreds of cheerleaders from around the country. Here she was in the center of Jessica's world, and she and Jessica weren't even speaking.

Elizabeth listened as the conversation swirled about her. The girls were all pumped up about the next day's events and were sizing up the competition.

"The Vermont girls look brutal," said Patty Gilbert, bringing a forkful of mashed potatoes to her lips. "They've got their routines timed to perfection."

Sara Eastbourne took a long gulp of lemonade. "And did you see the Texas Tigers, the team from San Antonio?"

"They came in second last year," put in Jeanie West. "I hear they're shoo-ins for the title this year."

"Not a chance," said Jessica, shaking her head firmly. "Not with us around."

"Oh, look, Heather," said Annie Whitman, pointing to the far corner of the cafeteria. "Your old squad from Reno is over there. Aren't you going to say hi?"

"No way." Heather snorted derisively. Annie raised one eyebrow and gave her an inquiring look.

Heather looked uncomfortable for a moment. "Well, they're the competition now," she explained, regaining her composure. "So, what do you think of the squad from Hawaii?" she asked, changing the subject quickly.

"They're not very impressive," said Lila with a dismissive wave of her hand. "I think they're just trying to win by looking good with their floral prints and colorful leis."

"That's true," agreed Amy. "They're pretty much all appearance and no substance."

"Yeah, but they have some great jumps," said Sandy Bacon.

"I saw them in a standing pyramid this afternoon," added Jade Wu.

Just then a stunning willowy girl with glossy brown hair appeared at the table. "Oh, hi," she said in a syrupy-sweet voice. "I just wanted to introduce myself. I'm Marissa James, the captain of the Reno squad. Heather here used to be on our team." The girls responded with a chorus of hellos.

"Hi, Marissa, long time no see," said Heather, smiling up at her. It seemed to Elizabeth that her smile didn't reach her eyes.

78

"How's it going, Heather?" said Marissa in a relaxed, friendly tone. "You know, it's just not the same at Reno since you, uh, since you—left."

"I'm sure," said Heather coolly. Heather sounded perfectly at ease, but the color seemed to drain from her face.

"You're the cocaptain, right?" said Marissa, leaning over to Elizabeth.

"Uh, no," said Elizabeth, her cheeks burning hotly. "My sister Jessica is the cocaptain." She indicated Jessica across the table.

"I think we met earlier at the bus," said Jessica in an unfriendly voice.

"Oh, did we?" said Marissa, showing no sign of recognition. "Well, you must be absolutely thrilled to be working with Heather," she said. "We really miss her at Reno. It's just not the same without her."

"I'm sure," said Jessica, her tone flat. "We really are thrilled to have her. Thrilled to pieces."

"Well, see you tomorrow." Marissa waved. "Good luck!"

"I hear she's the best cheerleader around," said Wilhemina as soon as Marissa was out of earshot.

"Yeah, everybody's been talking about her all day," added Peggy May. "She seems to have created quite a stir."

"She's definitely getting a lot of attention," put in Jeanie. "I saw a bunch of girls gathered around her earlier. It's like she's got a fan club."

"Well, I'm not surprised," said Maria. "She looks like a movie star."

79

Suddenly Heather scraped her chair back and stood up. "If you'll excuse me," she said, "I've got to get back to the cabin. I want to make sure our routine book for the weekend is in order." Annie opened her mouth to protest, but Heather was gone before she could say anything.

Elizabeth looked at her strangely as she left. Heather seemed to get all worked up whenever her old school was mentioned. Heather and Marissa must have a history, thought Elizabeth. Maybe Marissa hated working with her as much as Jessica did, she surmised.

A few minutes later Heather unlocked the door of the cabin and walked in alone, her heart pounding in her chest. She sat down hard on the bed and took a deep breath. Marissa James was going to try to make trouble for her, that was for sure. She'd been her greatest rival at Reno. Heather had been sole captain for two years in a row, and Marissa had despised her for it.

And to make it worse, the girls at Sweet Valley seemed overly interested in her history at Thomas Jefferson High. Especially Annie Whitman, who followed her around like a puppy. Heather looked at her watch. The girls would probably be back from dinner soon. If she went to bed early, they wouldn't be able to ask her any more questions, she decided.

Heather pulled down the covers on her bunk and gasped. Lying on her sheets was an ominous envelope across which her name was scrawled in bold black letters. Heather picked it up and opened it with shaking fingers. She pulled out a familiar newspaper clipping and stared at it unbelievingly, her whole body trembling. The headline read: "Kicky Captain Kicked Off Squad." Heather fell back on the bed and scanned the article:

Heather Mallone, the much celebrated captain of the Thomas Jefferson High cheerleading squad, who led her team to State for two years in a row, has been dismissed from the squad due to a serious cheating incident. The authorities involved—

Heather couldn't bear to read more. She crumpled up the article and threw it onto the ground. Her worst fear had been realized. She had tried so hard to keep her past a secret, and now it looked as if somebody wanted it to come out. Heather was desperate to keep her cheerleading history to herself. She would do anything, she thought—anything. She just had to find out who did this and what they wanted.

Thinking twice, Heather picked up the article from the floor and smoothed it out again. She folded it carefully and put it back in its envelope. Suddenly a piece of paper fluttered to the ground. Heather snatched it up. It was a note: "Meet me outside in the clearing tonight at ten. I'll be waiting." The note was signed Marissa James. Heather shivered and slipped the small piece of paper into her bag.

Chapter 7

"OK, guys, get ready to knock 'em dead!" exclaimed Jessica. The girls were in a huddle before the first competition on Saturday morning, and Jessica was giving them a pep talk. Everyone was wound up, and the excitement in the air was palpable. "Remember, arms straight, knees bent, chins up and out. And don't forget to smile, smile, smile."

All the girls put their arms in the middle of the circle, laying their hands on top of each other's. "One, two, three, SVH!" they yelled together. The girls let out a shout and threw their arms in the air.

"Girls, please take your seats in your sections in the bleachers!" came a booming voice over the loudspeaker. "Please take your seats! The first competition of the day will begin in fifteen minutes."

"All right, let's get moving!" said Heather in a

brassy tone, clapping her hands sharply. The girls followed as she led them to the Sweet Valley section in the stands. The competing squads were cordoned off in sections in the front half of the bleachers. The back half of the bleachers was devoted to members of the audience. The judges were lined up in special box seats in the front.

"Everybody's got today's program straight, right?" asked Jessica nervously as soon as they were all settled in the bleachers. The big moment had finally arrived, and she didn't want anything to go wrong. "We're doing the salsa routine first, the 'Mambo Jamba' this afternoon, and the 'Victory' combination at the end of the day."

"You've *got* to be kidding," said Heather, her voice dripping with disdain. "We're doing the salsa routine first?"

Jessica's temper flared. "Do you have a problem with that?" she demanded, her hands on her hips.

"Yes, I do," Heather asserted. "I think it's a mistake."

"And may I ask why?" Jessica asked, fixing Heather with a piercing stare.

"If we start out with the salsa routine, we're going to regret it," said Heather with a self-assured air. "I think we should do the 'Mambo Jamba' instead."

"I'm sure you do," said Jessica dryly. The salsa routine ended with a solo tumbling run by Jessica: a round-off followed by two back handsprings. The "Mambo Jamba," on the other hand, featured Heather's special combination jump. Obviously

Heather couldn't stand being out of the limelight for even one performance.

"The salsa routine is a nice upbeat number, but it's not technically complicated," Heather said. "The 'Mambo Jamba' is a showstopper. We'll catch the eyes of the judges right at the start."

"Heather, are you crazy?" asked Jessica in astonishment. "We can't just change the program at the last minute."

"Well, I made some last-minute adjustments last night," said Heather.

"Which you forgot to inform us about," said Jessica, folding her arms across her chest.

"I know, silly of me," said Heather, an apologetic smile on her face. "I didn't expect to fall asleep so fast."

"It's no big deal," said Patty Gilbert diplomatically. "We can just switch the order of the first two combinations."

"Look, guys," said Jessica. "It's our first performance, and we want to make a good impression. The salsa routine is our smoothest combination. We've been practicing it for weeks, and we've got it down to a science."

"Well, you know that first impressions are always the most important," said Heather. "If you want to play it safe and begin with a dud, that's fine with me. But I personally think we should start out with a bang."

"I'm for the 'Mambo Jamba,'" said Annie Whitman. "Heather's combination jump is the best we've got. Everybody will notice us from the start." Jessica fumed inwardly as Annie spoke.

"We'd better decide soon," said Elizabeth, looking at her watch nervously. "The competition starts in five minutes, and we're the third team to perform."

"Why don't we take a vote?" suggested Heather.

"Great idea!" said Annie.

Jessica gritted her teeth as Heather held the vote. "Whoever is in favor of the 'Mambo Jamba,' raise their hands," she said. Five sets of hands shot up immediately.

A small smile played on Jessica's lips as she counted the votes. It looked like seven to five in her favor. Then her smile faded as Maria, Sandy, and Jean slowly followed, lifting their arms awkwardly into the air. Only Lila, Amy, and Elizabeth's hands remained down. Jessica averted her eyes, feeling as if her friends had betrayed her.

"Well," said Heather, looking around with a self-satisfied smirk, "it looks like it's almost unanimous."

"OK, we'll start with the Mambo Jamba, then," said Jessica, swallowing her disappointment.

"Great!" Heather said. "I've got the tape right here."

What a coincidence, thought Jessica wryly as Heather jumped up and ran to the sound booth at the top of the bleachers to give the new tape to the controller.

Jessica stared at the field, seething in frustration. She barely noticed as the first two squads performed. Jessica didn't really care if they started with the "Mambo Jamba." It didn't matter to her one way or the other which combination they did first. But she was furious that Heather hadn't consulted her about it. And the squad had gone along with her, as usual. Heather just wanted to assert her power, thought Jessica in annoyance. And nobody even noticed it.

Jessica was so caught up in her thoughts that she didn't hear the announcer call their squad to the field.

"Jessica, c'mon!" urged Amy, by her side. "We're on!"

"Oh," said Jessica. She stood up and followed her squad down the bleachers, marching along with a stony look on her face.

"Jess," Amy said placatingly as they walked out to the field together, "Heather's jump is always a crowd pleaser, and she never, ever messes it up. It's guaranteed to win us this leg of the competition."

"All right, all right," Jessica grumbled, knowing deep down that Amy was probably right.

The girls took their positions in the center of the field and faced the judges. Suddenly the enormity of the situation hit her. They were about to perform in the first round of the national competition. Jessica stood tense and nervous as she waited for the music to start.

As the jazzy tune began to come through the loudspeaker, the girls began to move in time to the music; they swayed from side to side and lunged back and forth, shaking their pom-poms in the air. Jessica could feel the rhythm of the music throbbing through her body. Suddenly she forgot all about Heather and the audience and the judges. Her entire mind was filled with the pounding beat and the familiar steps.

Keeping in time with Jessica and Heather, the girls moved in perfect synchronicity. Jessica knew that they formed a uniform image, a whirlwind of fancy footwork and intricate moves. A hush seemed to sweep over the audience as the girls performed. The judges were motionless as well, riveted to the Sweet Valley High squad.

The beat changed, and the girls shifted to the athletic part of the program. They stood perfectly still for a beat, then launched into a series of side-by-side herkies. A round of applause greeted the difficult feat. Feeling a rush of adrenaline, the girls leaped into a trojan-crunch combination and followed it up with a spectacular team stag leap.

Jessica's mouth went dry as they approached the final, but most difficult, part of the program. She took a deep breath and leaped high into the air in a jumping split, dropping down to the ground on one knee, her pom-poms at her waist. Jade Wu followed, and in a wave pattern each girl leaped into the air in succession and dropped down to the earth. Jessica exhaled deeply as the last girl came down. Breathing heavily, the girls squatted on one knee in a line, their pom-poms held at their waists and radiant smiles on their faces.

Heather bounced up to the front of the group, getting in position for her combination jump. She stood poised and graceful in the middle of the field, commanding full attention. Suddenly she bounded across the field and jumped into the air in a perfect triple herky and Y-leap combination. As she landed, her foot slipped out from under her, and she tumbled across the field, somersaulting wildly. The crowd gasped audibly. Jessica sucked in her breath. She had never seen Heather make a mistake before. The judges jumped up to see if she was hurt. But like a pro, Heather got back up as if nothing had happened, continuing smoothly with the combination. She leaped into a series of energetic back flips. But her momentum seemed to give way before the last flip, preventing her from completing the rotation. Her arms flailed wildly, and she fell forward on her knees. Looking teary-eyed, she bounced up again and shot straight up in the air, landing in a crooked split.

A moment of silence followed the pathetic display, and then the crowd broke out into polite applause. The girls stood perfectly still, frozen smiles plastered on their faces.

"It's a disaster," Amy mumbled.

"A nightmare," agreed Lila.

"A total fiasco," said Jessica, speaking through clenched teeth, "and it's all Heather's fault."

"That was some night," Todd said, rubbing his neck as he maneuvered his BMW along the winding roads of the sleeping town on Saturday morning. The sun was just peeking out over the mountains, bathing the rustic landscape in a soft yellow glow.

"I feel like I've been through a war," agreed Ken, his voice still groggy with sleep. "We might as well have slept in a barracks." He yawned and stretched his arms above his head.

Todd felt as if he'd slept on a bed of Ping-Pong balls. The boys were all a little stiff from the lumpy beds at the Red Wood Hotel. They had arrived too late the evening before to go to the cheerleading compound, so they had found a hotel and called it a night.

"I think I'm going to be sick," complained Winston from the backseat of the car.

"Here, Winston, have some of these," said Ken, handing Winston a half-eaten bag of potato chips.

"Ugh, don't even put that near me," said Winston. The gallon of mocha-chip ice cream the boys had consumed on their way down wasn't helping matters, Todd thought. Their lack of sleep was compounded by collective bellyaches.

"I'll never eat again!" Winston vowed, raising his index finger in the air.

"At least not until lunchtime," said Ken with a laugh.

"Well, it's time to rally!" said Todd, flipping on the radio and picking up the speed. Despite his aching body and delicate stomach, Todd's spirits were soaring. In just a few minutes he would see Elizabeth again. He would finally have the chance to patch things up with her. He was also looking forward to watching the squad perform at the national competition.

"I can't wait to see the girls show their stuff," said Todd, voicing his thoughts aloud.

"Me neither," agreed Ken. "I'm psyched that we'll be there. The cheerleaders have been supporting our teams for years. It'll be nice to cheer them on for a change."

"I wonder if the competitions have started yet," mused Winston.

"I don't know, but we'll soon find out," said Todd excitedly as he spotted a huge stone arch marking the entranceway of the cheerleading compound. "That's it up ahead!" he said, pointing to the gates.

Todd cut his speed and coasted up the road to the entrance. Suddenly he pulled the car to a screeching halt. A foreboding placard greeted their arrival. The sign read: NO BOYS ALLOWED ON THE NATIONAL CHAMPIONSHIP GROUNDS.

"Oh, no!" despaired Todd.

"That's impossible!" lamented Ken.

"But that's discrimination!" protested Winston.

"That's right," said Todd in a determined voice. "And we're not going to let them get away with it." Todd wasn't exactly sure how they were going to do that, but he was sure they'd think of something. They had come too far to leave without putting up a fight.

"Follow me, men," said Todd, cutting the engine and hopping out of the car. Ken and Winston jumped out as well, and the three of them approached the entrance. Two official-looking guards in matching uniforms stood in front of the gates.

"Can I help you, boys?" asked one of the guards, a thin-faced man with a fuzzy mustache.

"Yes, sir," said Ken politely. "We're here to observe the competition."

"Can't you read?" asked the other guard in a gruff tone. His feet were planted widely on the ground, and his crossed arms rested lazily on his big belly.

"Sorry, fellows," said the first guard in a kindlier tone, "but no boys are permitted on the grounds during the national competition."

"But that's not fair!" protested Winston. "It's illegal to discriminate on grounds of race or gender."

"This ain't a job interview," said the second guard in a surly voice. "Boys don't belong at a girls' event. They just make trouble and mess everything up."

Todd thought quickly. "Well, actually, we're reporters for the *Hollywood Globe*," he said. He addressed his words to the first guard, who looked like the more reasonable of the two. "We've been assigned the national championship to cover for this week's front-page story."

"I see," he said, his expression dubious. He paused to think for a moment, twirling his mustache between his fingers.

Todd waited breathlessly for his response. Trying to look authentic, Ken quickly pulled his camera out of his backpack and began shooting pictures of the compound.

"Well," said the guard finally, rubbing his jaw

91

thoughtfully, "I'm sure the editors of your newspaper will understand when you explain the situation to them."

"You know, sir," Todd said, taking another stab at it, "this kind of coverage would be great press for the national championships."

"It would lend new prestige to the entire sport," added Ken for good measure.

"All right," said the guard. "Let's see your press passes."

"Press passes?" Todd repeated dumbly.

"As in ID cards for the *Hollywood Globe*," said the burly guard.

Todd gulped and looked at his friends for help. Ken jumped in and took over. "We left our press passes back at the office," he said smoothly, "and we'll be sure to bring them by later. But the thing is, we've really got to get into the compound now."

Todd decided to make a personal appeal. "You see, our girlfriends are in there," he said. "And we've got to see them. It's urgent."

The guards weren't impressed.

"Somehow I don't think that counts as an emergency," said the first guard, clearly getting impatient. "And I think your girlfriends are cheerleaders just like you're reporters for the *Hollywood Globe*."

"What's wrong, sonny?" asked the second guard, his jowly face leering. "Aren't there enough girls for you back in your high school?"

Todd opened his mouth to argue further, but the second guard waved him off. "Read my lips," he said, his voice slow and condescending. *"No— boys—allowed!"*

"I can't believe it," Jessica said, pacing back and forth in one of the spare rooms of the lodge late Saturday morning. "First Heather screws up and then she disappears." Heather had run off immediately following the first competition. Annie was gone as well. As soon as Heather had left, Annie had jumped up and followed her off the field, calling, "Heather! Heather!" Jessica shook her head. Annie's idol worship was really revolting.

"Do you want me to go find her?" asked Maria.

"No, we're better off without her," said Jessica, dismissing the suggestion with a wave of her hand. "Now," she said, facing the girls and rubbing her hands together. "We've got some important decisions to make. We're in a critical situation—an *extremely* critical situation."

For once Elizabeth had to agree with Jessica. The girls had been ranked fiftieth after the first competition. Jessica had called an emergency meeting immediately following the morning's fiasco.

"It's worse than critical," lamented Sandy Bacon dramatically. "It's the end of the world."

"We're going to be the laughingstock of the entire school," said Sara Eastbourne, flopping down on a couch on her back.

"We're ruined," echoed Jean West. "All our hard work for nothing. Hours and hours of practice. Days and days of preparation. And then—*poof!*"

93

She snapped her fingers in the air. "Two minutes, and it's all over."

"It's all over, is it?" Jessica said. Elizabeth looked at her sister suspiciously. Jessica had a familiar look in her eye. A look that meant trouble. Elizabeth could almost see the wheels clicking in Jessica's head. The morning's competition had been a total disaster, but Jessica wasn't one to give in easily. This was the first time the squad had met together without Heather, and Elizabeth was sure Jessica would find a way to turn the situation to her advantage.

"So you all just want to give up, huh?" said Jessica, fixing the girls with a challenging stare. "One setback and you just want to throw in the towel. Is that right, Jeanie?" Jessica asked, giving the girl a hard look.

"No, of course not," said Jeanie defensively.

"Is that what kind of team we are?" Jessica said, addressing all of them.

"No!" chorused the girls.

"Does the Sweet Valley High team just accept defeat without a fight?" said Jessica.

"No way!" yelled the girls, getting riled up.

"Who's number one?" shouted Jessica.

"SVH!" they yelled together.

"That's the spirit," said Jessica, her face breaking into a broad grin. She sat down on the floor and spoke quietly. "Now, I've got a plan," Jessica said. The girls gathered around and looked at her expectantly. "It's simple, but it'll work."

"Well?" Lila asked impatiently, tapping her cherry-red fingernails on the ottoman.

"We performed beautifully today, right?" said Jessica.

"Except for Heather's jumps," said Sandy.

"Or attempts at jumps," qualified Maria.

"Exactly," said Jessica. "So I hereby raise an official motion to have Heather voted off the squad. She's obviously collapsing under all the pressure. Right now we've still got a chance. We've got six more competitions to go. Either we make a comeback, or we let Heather bring us down."

Elizabeth's mouth dropped open. Jessica had protested wildly when Heather had kicked Maria and Sandy off the squad, and rightly so. And now here she was suggesting the same thing.

"I'm with Jessica," said Amy.

"Me too," agreed Lila.

"All in favor?" asked Jessica. Jessica looked around in satisfaction as one by one all the girls raised their hands. All except Elizabeth.

Jessica turned furious eyes to her sister, willing her to go along with the group. But Elizabeth refused to be bullied. "I'm not in favor!" she proclaimed, jumping up and facing the girls.

"We're a team, and the whole point of being a team is that you stick together," said Elizabeth, speaking in a strong voice. She addressed her words not to Jessica, but to the rest of the girls. "A squad is about good sportsmanship and camaraderie, about teamwork and solidarity."

The girls seemed distinctly uncomfortable as Elizabeth made her speech. Maria and Sandy fidgeted nervously; Jade and Patty stared down at the ground; Lila traced patterns in the woodwork with a finger.

"When you're a team, you stick together through thick and thin, and you don't kick people when they're down," Elizabeth continued, her voice becoming more impassioned as she spoke. "If we're not going to act like a team, then a title doesn't mean anything."

"Liz is right," said Maria, hanging her head. "Sandy and I were devastated when Heather kicked us off the squad."

"Yeah, you can't just throw people out if they make a mistake," Sandy put in.

The whole team begrudgingly agreed.

Jessica stood up. "We're going to regret this," she said, addressing the squad as a whole, but glaring at Elizabeth. "Mark my words, we're going to regret this." With that, she pivoted on her heel and marched out of the room.

"Man, I can't believe it!" said Todd, hitting his hand against the dashboard for the tenth time as the boys headed back to Sweet Valley on Saturday. He felt like screaming in frustration. They'd come all that way for nothing. "No boys allowed!" he said, shaking his head. "No boys allowed!"

"You can say that again!" said Winston with a grin. Todd smiled in spite of himself. He had been repeating "No boys allowed!" like a mantra for the last hour.

"No-o! Not again!" yelled Ken, making a motion to hang himself.

"What a total waste of time," Todd said in disgust.

"And money," added Ken.

"And ice cream," lamented Winston.

"How can they not allow boys in?" asked Todd, outraged. "Who could be in the audience?"

"A bunch of retired cheerleaders," said Ken.

"Or grade-school cheerleader wanna-bes," said Todd.

"Maybe they think we'd be a distraction," suggested Winston.

"Well, I can see that," said Ken. "After all, who could resist us?"

The boys lapsed into silence as Todd steered his black BMW down the busy Pacific Coast Highway. The blue-green ocean glittered off to their right in the distance, seagulls white specks on the horizon.

"Are we almost there?" asked Winston a few minutes later, shifting his lanky frame uncomfortably in the backseat.

"I think we're about halfway home," said Todd, trying to make out the road sign ahead of him. He managed to read the sign as they passed it. The sign said Cheer Ahead.

Suddenly Todd recalled the Cheer Ahead catalog he had seen at the Wakefields, the catalog from which Jessica had chosen the squad's uniforms. He slammed on the brakes. The car lurched forward, and the boys flew back against the seats.

"Oh, no!" said Winston.

"Oh, yes!" said Todd.

"Brilliant idea," said Ken.

      ❁   ❁   ❁

"OK, you guys, now don't let this morning get you down," Jessica said, giving the girls a little pep talk before the second round of the competition on Saturday. "This routine features my jump," she reassured them, smiling sweetly at Heather, "so we won't have to worry about any mishaps."

For once Heather looked at a loss for words. She opened her mouth as if to respond but shut it quickly, looking the other way.

"And performing next is the squad from Sweet Valley, California!" boomed the announcer's voice.

"We're on!" said Maria.

"C'mon, guys!" Jessica said, running out to the field. The girls followed her enthusiastically, waving their pom-poms in the air.

Once in the center of the field, they spread out in a line, positioning themselves at arm's length from one other. As the lively samba beat began to pour out of the speakers, the girls started clapping their hands rhythmically in time with the music.

"How're we feelin?" Jessica yelled.

"Feelin' hot, hot, hot!" shouted the girls, stomping their feet and chanting with the music.

"How're you feeling?" Jessica roared, cupping her ear to the audience.

"Feelin' hot, hot, hot!" responded the crowd.

Fueled on by the audience's enthusiasm, the girls moved through the salsa routine flawlessly, shifting from jump to jump without a hitch. As the beat picked up, they sashayed into a jazzy dance number, swaying their hips and waving their arms in the air like flamenco dancers. The audience clapped along as the girls pranced across the field, performing an impressive display of fancy footwork.

Moving into position for their final jump, all the girls except Jessica leaped into the air at the same time and landed in Chinese splits with their feet touching. From an aerial view the girls formed a six-point star. A chorus of *oohs* and *aahs* could be heard from the crowd as they observed the star formation.

Jessica took a deep breath as she moved into position for her final jump: a tumbling run followed by a side-kick, Y-leap combination. Jessica tensed the muscles in her legs and sprang into action, moving through the jump flawlessly. The crowd burst into spontaneous applause as she finished the combination, hurtling her body high into the air in a Y leap and landing in the center of the star in a split.

The girls brought their legs together in unison and bent their knees. Jumping up, they moved into position for their final move: a five-four-three pyramid, their most impressive maneuver. "We've got the fever, we're hot, we can't be stopped!" chanted the girls, clapping and shouting as they hoisted each other onto their shoulders. Hopping up adeptly, Jessica, Elizabeth, and Patty climbed up the first two tiers and positioned themselves on top. Patty knelt in the middle, her pom-poms raised high. Balancing on one knee, Jessica and Elizabeth raised their arms in the air in L shapes.

"SVH!" yelled the girls. "We're hot, hot, hot!" The crowd roared its approval. Suddenly Jessica felt the pyramid sway. Out of the corner of her eye she saw Heather collapse at the bottom, causing a domino effect. One by one the girls fell. Finally the whole pyramid collapsed on top of Heather, and the girls toppled in a heap onto the ground.

The girls scrambled up and took their final positions, holding their heads high as the judges ranked them. Jessica stared unseeing at the bleachers, blinking back tears from her eyes. She had never been so mortified in all her life.

"I'm so sorry," Heather gasped out as they took their seats in the stands, a stricken look on her face. "It was an accident."

"Don't worry about it, Heather," said Annie, patting her hand in a comforting manner. "It could happen to any of us."

"But it didn't," Heather said, choking back a sob. "I'm so humiliated!" She jumped up and ran from the field, tears streaming down her face.

But Jessica didn't buy any of it. Heather wasn't humiliated. She was trying to humiliate Jessica. And it was working. It was clear as day what Heather was doing. She was deliberately sabotaging the competition just to make Jessica look bad. Jessica shook her head in amazement. She knew Heather was cutthroat, but she never thought she'd go this far for a personal vendetta. She would have never dreamed that Heather would sacrifice the entire competition just to embarrass her.

The girls quieted down as the judges read out

their scores: artistic impression: 20; school spirit: 25; athletic ability: 10; tumbling: 10. The color drained from Jessica's face as she digested the information. They had received a point total of 65 out of 100, one of the lowest scores of the day.

Shaking with suppressed fury, Jessica forced herself to look at the electronic scoreboard at the far end of the field. She scanned it quickly, her heart sinking as she made her way farther and farther down the list. Finally she spotted their squad listed third from the bottom. Jessica buried her head in her hands. Sweet Valley High was ranked forty-eighth in the competition.

"Don't go anywhere yet," Jessica said a moment later, addressing the squad. She wasn't planning to give up yet. It was time to take matters into her own hands. "I want everybody on the south side of the practice field immediately for a run-through of the 'Victory' combination. We're going to whip ourselves into shape for the next competition."

The girls begrudgingly stood up, grumbling among themselves. "Oh, what's the use?" Maria said. "We might as well throw in the towel now," muttered Sara. "Yeah, quitting's more respectable than losing," added Jean.

"Oh, one more thing," Jessica added as the girls began to trudge down the bleachers. They stopped and looked back. "I want to rechoreograph the final jump of the 'Victory' routine. Can somebody get the routine book from the cabin?"

"I'll go," Elizabeth offered, looking just as dejected as the rest of them.

Five minutes later the girls were gathered in the grass, going through the motions of stretching out and limbering up. They were a motley crew, thought Jessica, surveying the group. Shoulders sagging, Sara turned her head from side to side, stretching out her neck muscles. Amy sat spread-eagle, facedown in the grass with her arms stretched out in front of her. Jade and Patty were positioned directly across from each other for a dual stretch. Legs spread and toes touching, they moved as if rowing a boat in slow motion, slowly pulling the other down to the ground. Jean, Sandy, and Maria didn't even bother to make an effort. They lay flat on their backs on the grass, staring up at the sky in silence.

"OK, that's enough for now!" said Jessica, clapping her hands together. She gathered everybody around her.

"Girls," said Jessica, getting right to the point, "the situation is getting dire. There's only one problem at this point."

"Heather Mallone," supplied Amy.

Jessica nodded. "And there's only one solution."

"Can Heather," said Lila.

"Exactly," agreed Jessica.

"But we can't just cut Heather!" exclaimed Annie. "She's done so much for us. She brought a whole new approach to the squad—new cheers, new uniforms."

"Yeah," agreed Jade. "Heather makes us stand out."

102

"Well, the only way she's making us stand out now is by humiliating us," put in Amy.

"I don't know what kind of spell that girl has cast on you guys," Jessica said, her voice firm, "but if you remember, the ACA representative chose both my squad and Heather's squad to go to nationals. My squad stood out on its own—without Heather."

"Jessica's right," Lila chimed in. "The squads tied at the cheer-off."

"Well, what about what Elizabeth said?" worried Maria. "About team spirit and camaraderie?"

"And about sticking together when you're down?" added Sandy.

"Look, guys," said Jessica. "We gave Heather a second chance, and she blew it. I don't know what she's up to, but I don't think she's worried about team spirit at this point."

"Are you saying that Heather's doing this on purpose?" said Annie hotly. "She'd never do that."

"I'm not saying anything," said Jessica. "All I'm saying is that we have two choices at this point: We leave Heather in and we come in last place, or we get rid of her and do respectably, maybe even place. There's still time, you know. Now—all in favor?"

All the girls raised their hands, solemn looks on their faces. Annie hesitated and looked around, then slowly lifted her hand in the air.

"Looks like the ayes have it," said Lila.

"Good," Jessica said, rubbing her hands together. "It's decided, then. Heather's off the squad."

"But what do we do now?" asked Jeanie. "We haven't got a chance after the first two—"

Jessica held up a hand, cutting her off. "Now," she said, her eyes gleaming, "it's time to make our comeback."

Chapter 8

"I can't believe I'm shaving my legs, I can't believe I'm shaving my legs," Winston moaned again and again, holding a foamy, furry leg underneath the bathtub faucet. He brought the pink razor slowly up his muscular calf, wincing as clumps of hair fell into the tub.

It was Saturday afternoon, and the boys were back at the hotel, ready to don their new cheerleading costumes.

"Darnit!" Todd muttered as he poked himself in the eye with a mascara stick. He stood at the bathroom mirror, meticulously applying makeup. An array of cosmetics was splayed across the bathroom counter. Todd stood back and surveyed his handiwork. Something wasn't quite right.

"How did I let myself get talked into this?" Winston wondered aloud.

"Don't worry, Winston, it's all for a good cause," Todd reassured him.

"A good cause! A good cause!" mumbled Winston. "No cause is worth the hair on my legs." He held up a smooth white calf and moaned.

Todd squinted into the mirror, trying to ascertain the problem. The eyes, he decided finally, that was it. They needed a touch of color. He fumbled through the confusing assortment of jars, tubes, and ointments laid out on the counter. "Ken!" Todd said. "Can I borrow your blue eyeshadow?"

"Coming!" Ken called in a falsetto voice. A moment later he sashayed into the bathroom like a runway model, adorned in a classic cheerleading costume. "How do I look, dah-lings?" Ken drawled, his hands on his hips. He pirouetted slowly, pausing to exhibit the cheerleading outfit from a variety of angles. It was bright purple and yellow, with a V-necked sweater and a pleated skirt. A big, gold *S* was emblazoned on the sweater. Ken whirled in a circle, displaying the flare of the skirt.

Todd put his fingers to his lips and let out an approving whistle.

"Hubba, hubba!" said Winston, twisting around to watch the show.

"I always knew you'd make a great girl," said Todd with a grin.

"Here's your eyeshadow, honey," said Ken, batting his eyelashes at Todd. "But make sure to return it!" He pressed the compact into Todd's hand.

Suddenly Ken jumped with fright as he looked into Todd's face. He stood back and stared, his mouth agape.

Winston followed Ken's gaze. "Oh-mi-god!" he exclaimed.

"What, what?" Todd asked, looking from one to the other. Winston was staring openmouthed, and Ken had a look of horror on his face.

"Uh, Todd, we're trying to be cheerleaders, not cabaret dancers," Ken said.

"What do you mean?" Todd asked, studying his face in the mirror. He had outlined the rims of his eyes with a thick layer of purple eyeliner, creating the effect of a somewhat soulful raccoon face. The eyeliner then extended outward, curling upward from his lids to his brows. Thick layers of mascara coated his lashes, which sprung out like spider's legs. Two sharp lines of bright-pink blush highlighted his prominent cheekbones, and scarlet lipstick outlined his full, penciled lips.

"Oh, do you think I overdid it a bit?" Todd asked, biting his lip. He coughed as he tasted the artificial candy taste of lipstick on his tongue.

"Overdid it is being kind," said Ken.

"I think 'garish' is the word you're looking for," Winston added.

Todd's face fell. At this rate they'd never get to the cheerleading compound. There was no way they'd fool the guards. "I'm just not cut out for this," Todd said, throwing his arms into the air.

"OK, Todd, baby, don't despair. We're going to do you over." Ken fished around the counter and came up with a jar of makeup remover. He handed Todd the cream and a washcloth. "Now, first of all, get this stuff off."

Ken fiddled around with the makeup as Todd wiped gobs of it off his face. "Now, stick with me," Ken said, readying a jar of mauve blush and a makeup brush, "and we'll have you looking lovely in no time."

Jessica marched back to the cabin after her meeting with the girls, a determined air in her gait. Pine needles crackled underneath her feet as she strode through the woods, taking a circuitous route. She was going back to the cabin to break the news to Heather, and she didn't want to meet Elizabeth on the way.

Jessica practiced her speech in her head. "Heather, I've got some news for you," she said aloud. "The squad held a meeting, and we decided that it might be better for all of us if you agreed to sacrifice your position on the squad for the good of the team." No, too pointed. Heather wouldn't appreciate having her own words thrown in her face, and Jessica needed her cooperation. She tried a different tack. "Heather, maybe you shouldn't bother showing up for the competition this evening." Nah, too subtle. She might as well be direct. "Heather, you're off the squad." Jessica smiled as she repeated the words. She liked the sound of it.

Jessica was sure that Heather was going to put up a major fight, but she wasn't going to budge. According to the cheerleading bylaws, one cocaptain had complete autonomy in the absence of the other. In fact, when Jessica had protested after Heather had kicked Sandy and Maria off the

108

squad, Heather had thrown that rule in her face. Well, she was going to get a taste of her own medicine now, thought Jessica in satisfaction. The squad had voted unanimously to kick Heather off the squad, and that was that. Jessica had followed the rules to a *T*, and there was nothing Heather could do about it.

The only problem was Elizabeth, thought Jessica as she climbed up the steep hill to the cabin. Jessica had left immediately following her pep talk, hoping to avoid Elizabeth until the third competition. She had left the girls in Lila's hands to run through the "Victory" routine. Fortunately, Elizabeth hadn't returned to the field in time. And Jessica hoped she had already left the cabin.

"Heather?" Jessica called, pushing open the wooden door of Hunter House.

"Hmm?" Heather said, turning her head. She was sitting in her bunk in the dark, her knees pulled up to her chest and her arms wrapped around them.

"We have to talk," Jessica said, marching into the room and flicking on the overhead light, a bulb hanging from a string in the peaked wooden ceiling.

"Sure," Heather said, blinking at the light. Her face was tear streaked and her eyes were red and puffy.

"Where's Elizabeth?" asked Jessica, looking around the room.

"She left a while ago," Heather said. "She was just here to pick something up."

"Good," Jessica said, pacing across the room, trying to determine how to handle the situation. She decided to get right to the point. "Heather, the squad took a vote this afternoon, and we voted unanimously to kick you off the team."

Heather opened her mouth, but Jessica went on. "And there's nothing you can do about it," she continued, fire in her eyes. "We aren't going to let you deliberately sabotage the SVH competition. The other girls may believe you've made some honest mistakes, but I know better. Your attempt to make me look foolish just isn't—"

"Jessica!" Heather interrupted her. Jessica's whole body tensed as she stopped to face her, anticipating a fight.

"It's fine," Heather said, waving a dismissive hand. "No problem."

Jessica looked at her suspiciously.

"Really," Heather said. "Don't worry about it."

"But—" Jessica sputtered, unable to believe her ears.

"Now, do you think I could be alone?" asked Heather gruffly, turning her back on Jessica.

"Uh, sure," said Jessica, turning out the light and walking out the door. How could Heather have made such a sudden about-face? wondered Jessica incredulously as she made her way back to the practice field.

"We were great!" Jessica enthused, slinging an arm around Lila and Amy as the girls walked to the cafeteria for dinner. They had just completed the

110

third round, which sealed the first leg of the competition. The "Victory" routine had gone off without a hitch. They had cut Heather's jump from the end, and it hadn't even been noticed. The Sweet Valley High squad had come in fifth, boosting their overall ratings from forty-eighth to thirty-fifth place.

"Yeah, we're back on track!" agreed Amy. All the girls' spirits seemed visibly higher.

"We're on our way to vic-tory!" said Maria, performing the steps with which they had finished their routine. "S-U-C-C-E-S-S, that's the way we spell success!" she called out.

"V-I-C-T-O-R-Y, that's Sweet Valley's victory cry!" yelled Sandy and Jean. The three girls jumped into the air in a double herky and held their arms up in a V formation.

"I hate to put a damper on things," said Jade Wu, "but I don't think we stand a chance."

"What do you mean?" asked Maria in surprise.

"We may have been good, but we weren't good enough," said Jade, shaking her head. "If we want to place in the competition, we have to win every event."

"But we were perfect," protested Amy. "We executed every step flawlessly."

"Look, guys, let's face it," said Jade in a matter-of-fact tone, "without Heather we're ordinary."

Jessica wheeled on her. "What are you saying?" she demanded hotly, her arms folded across her chest.

Jade looked visibly uncomfortable. "I mean, we're

ordinary without Heather—just like without *you* we'd be ordinary," she said, trying to make amends.

"Well, I don't think we're ordinary," said Jessica in a huff. "And that kind of attitude isn't going to get us anywhere!" She stormed away from Jade and stalked toward the lodge alone.

Suddenly Jessica heard footsteps approaching from behind her. Elizabeth was marching up to her, a furious look on her face. Apparently Elizabeth had decided to break their vow of silence.

"How dare you make a unanimous decision without consulting me first!" Elizabeth ranted as she reached her. "How dare you hold a meeting and vote without me!"

"I didn't hold a meeting without you, Liz," Jessica scoffed. "You chose to go back to the cabin."

Elizabeth's eyes narrowed. "Jessica, you are as transparent as Plexiglas. You knew I'd offer to go back, and you made sure to vote without me."

"Oh, Liz, that's ridiculous," sneered Jessica. "Don't you think you're being a bit paranoid?"

"No, I don't!" said Elizabeth hotly. "I am sick and tired of being manipulated by you. It's totally against the cheerleading bylaws to make a squad decision without all the members present."

"So what do you want to do about it?" asked Jessica.

"I demand a revote!" Elizabeth said. "And if you don't agree, I'll take it to the head of the ACA!"

"Well, Liz, I don't think that's going to get you too far," said Jessica.

"And why not?" Elizabeth asked, sparks flying from her eyes. The two girls stopped and faced each other in open confrontation, identical icy stares coming from identical blue-green eyes.

"Because it's too late now, that's why," said Jessica. "I already told Heather about it, and she agreed not to be on the squad."

Elizabeth's mouth dropped open. "Heather agreed?!"

"That's right, Liz," said Jessica. "She wants to sacrifice her position in order to save the team."

Elizabeth was speechless. "Now, if you'll excuse me," said Jessica, brushing past her sister, "I'm kind of hungry."

"OK, just act natural," Todd said as the three boys padded across the grounds in full cheerleading regalia. They were outfitted in their purple-and-gold cheerleading costumes, complete with big white Keds and women's wigs.

"Oh, no problem," said Winston. "I *feel* natural. Only usually I prefer a sheerer shade of lipstick!"

Todd had to agree with Winston. He had never felt so awkward—or so ridiculous—in his whole life. But it looked as though their disguises were working so far. The boys had passed through the gates without incident. The guards had just waved them on.

A gust of wind blew up, and Ken raised his hand to his head, holding his wig in place. "Oh, did I mess up my hair?" he said.

Todd paused to check out Ken's wild, curly blond mane. "Not a strand out of place," he reassured him. "Your locks look lovely."

"And you make a fabulous brunette," Ken said.

"What about me, guys?" asked Winston, putting a hand to his short red bob.

Todd tried not to laugh as he took in Winston's attire. Winston's costume looked just like Todd's and Ken's, but his sweater had glittery sequins on it, as well as feather trim along the neckline. The store had run out of standard costumes, and Winston had had to take a special one.

"Well," Ken said diplomatically, "you won't win any beauty contests, but it works."

"I think that's the field up ahead," Todd said, pointing in front of him.

"I don't think I can go through with this," Winston said suddenly. "They're going to laugh us off the grounds."

Todd stepped back to survey Ken and Winston. "You guys look great," he said.

"You mean, you girls," corrected Ken.

"Right," said Todd, nodding. "From a distance you'd never suspect anything. You look like normal cheerleaders." Todd cocked his head to the side. "A little large, but besides that—"

"Well, here goes nothing," said Winston, taking a deep breath. They walked daintily under the bleachers and onto the field. It looked as if the stands were emptying out.

"Excuse me," Todd said in a feminine voice, stopping two girls, a blonde and a brunette, with big green *H's* monographed on their sweaters. "When is the next competition?"

The dark-haired girl looked at him strangely. "They're all over for the day," she said.

"We're all going to the lodge for dinner," said the blonde, looking the boys up and down.

"See you later!" said the brunette with a giggle, bouncing off with her girlfriend.

"Darnit!" Todd said. "We missed the competition."

"All dressed up and nowhere to go," lamented Ken.

"Do you see any of the SVH squad?" asked Todd, looking around the field. The boys scanned the field rapidly. Cheerleaders were milling about, but there was no sign of any of the Sweet Valley High cheerleaders.

"There are some girls in red-and-white uniforms down there," Todd said, shading his eyes from the glare of the setting sun.

"Nah, I don't think that's them," said Ken, squinting in the direction Todd indicated. "I don't recognize any girls from the squad."

"Excuse me, are you girls registered?" came an ominous voice from behind them.

The boys wheeled around to find an athletic-looking woman dressed in a blue suit. Todd gasped as he read the tag on the woman's jacket: Zoe Balsam, Director, ACA. They were face-to-face with the head of the American Cheerleading Association. Todd's heart began sounding a drumroll. It looked as if their visit to the American

Cheerleading Compound was going to be a short one.

"Uh, no, ma'am," squeaked Winston in a falsetto voice, patting his hair into place.

"Every cheerleading squad has to check in," said Ms. Balsam. "The security is extremely tight on the premises." A quizzical look crossed her face, and she scanned the list she held in her hands. "In fact, you can't compete without registering."

"We're just here to watch," explained Todd, putting his hands on his hips and adopting a feminine posture.

The woman looked at them suspiciously. "I haven't seen you girls yet. What are your names?"

"Uh, I'm Tilda Wilkins," said Todd, "and these are my squadmates, Kendall Matthews and . . ." Todd's voice trailed off as he searched for an appropriate name.

"I'm Winnie Egbert," said Winston, extending a dainty hand.

The woman still looked dubious as she shook Winston's hand. "And where are you from?" she asked.

"Uhh—" Ken stuttered, looking down at his sweater. "Sss—"

"Saskatchewan," Todd said, taking over. "We're from Saskatchewan, Canada."

"Well, girls, whether you're here to compete, train, or observe, you've got to be registered," said the director sternly.

"Yes, ma'am," said Ken. The boys turned and began briskly walking away.

"Girls!" yelled Ms. Balsam a few moments later.

"Oh, boy," muttered Winston. Todd held his breath as they looked back, waiting for her to blow the whistle on them.

"Registration's that way," she said, pointing to the right.

The boys quickly changed course and ran in the other direction, falling over one another in their haste. Todd risked a look back. Ms. Balsam was just standing there looking after them, shaking her head.

Chapter 9

"This way!" called Jessica, leading the squad in a run through the woods of the cheerleading compound early Sunday morning. The trail forked ahead of her, and she turned to the right, choosing a rigorous uphill path. The girls formed a procession as they followed the narrow trail through the dense redwoods. Lila ran directly behind Jessica, and Elizabeth brought up the rear.

The girls jogged along in silence for a few minutes as they maneuvered the difficult trail. The early-morning air was fresh and misty, and the sky was a clear gray-blue. All that could be heard in the stillness of the morning was the girls' breathing and the sounds of nature. Birds warbled and chirped, and a variety of invisible insects buzzed noisily. An occasional twig snapped as the girls trod upon the dewy earth.

Jessica breathed in the fresh air with satisfaction,

her aquamarine eyes bright with excitement. She was thrilled to have full control of the squad again. She had two days to lead the team to victory, and she was determined to do it. The squad had been up training since seven A.M. They had started with stretching exercises in the practice field and had followed up with a half hour of low-impact aerobic exercise. If they wanted to win all the competitions of the day, they had to be in the finest shape possible.

"I think—I'm—going—to pass out," panted Lila dramatically from behind Jessica.

"Have some water," offered Maria, passing forth a plastic canteen of fresh springwater.

"Thanks," breathed Lila, taking a long gulp as she jogged along the path. She wiped her brow with the arm of her T-shirt and passed the jug back.

"Water!" Jean cried from the back of the line. The girls handed the canteen down the line, each taking a swig in turn.

"Hey, Jess!" Lila called, adjusting the purple sweatband around her forehead to keep her hair off her face.

"Yeah?" Jessica asked, jogging along at a brisk pace.

"I think we need some inspiration," Lila said.

"Inspiration coming up," Jessica returned. The trail opened out into a grassy clearing in the woods. Jessica reduced her speed and trotted out into the meadow.

"Freedom!" exclaimed Maria, bouncing into a series of cartwheels in the clearing.

"Where—does she—get the—energy?" panted Amy, coming up to join Lila.

"Don't worry, the worst is over," Jessica encouraged the group, jogging along at a constant pace. "You guys are doing great! Now, everybody sing along!"

The girls clumped together as they left the woods, running in groups of twos and threes.

"I don't know but I been told!" yelled out Jessica.

"I don't know but I been told!" chorused the girls.

"SVH is good as gold!" shouted Jessica.

"SVH is good as gold!" returned the girls.

"I don't know, but it's been said!" chanted Jessica.

"I don't know but it's been said!" repeated the girls.

"The number one team's the white and red!" yelled Jessica.

"The number one team's the white and red!" echoed the girls.

"Sound off, sound off, YEAH!!" The girls cheered together, infused with new energy as they ran through the meadow.

Jessica clapped her hands together and took off toward the forest on the opposite side of the clearing. "I don't know but it's been said . . ." she yelled.

"Hey, I think I see them!" exclaimed Todd, catching a glimpse of the Sweet Valley High squad through the redwoods across the meadow. Todd,

Ken, and Winston, still in their cheerleading outfits, were jogging through the forest in search of
the girls. They had been trailing them all morning.
After catching sight of them leaving the practice
field earlier, the boys had followed them at a distance into the woods.

"Are you sure that's them?" Ken asked, running
up to Todd's side. His skirt whipped up in the wind
and flew around his waist. "Yikes!" Ken exclaimed,
patting it down quickly.

Todd peered through the trees, trying to make
out the figures in the woods. All he could see was
a blur of sweatpants and T-shirts. Perspiration
trickled down his cheek, and Todd wiped it off
with the back of his hand, smudging his makeup
across his face.

"All my hard work!" Ken joked as he noticed
the blotchy mess covering Todd's face.

"Ugh," Todd said, looking at the creamy pink
blur on the back of his hand. "I don't know how
girls can stand wearing all this gunk on their faces."

"It's one of the great unsolved mysteries,"
agreed Ken.

Suddenly the sounds of chanting wafted in their
direction. The words were faint but distinct. *"I
don't know but I been told!"* they heard.

"That's Jessica!" exclaimed Ken.

"C'mon!" Todd yelled, waving at Ken. The boys
ran out into the meadow toward the forest opposite. They stopped and looked around them
quickly. There was no sign of the girls anywhere.

"Shh!" said Ken, listening carefully. A faint

sound of chanting came from the far end of the forest.

"Follow the voices!" said Todd, taking off in the direction of the singing. The boys raced after him, trying to trace the sound of the girls' singing.

Fifteen minutes later they found themselves at their point of departure.

"We're in a maze," said Ken, shaking his head.

"The wind must throw the sound," said Winston.

"We'll never find them now," said Todd in a dejected tone, looking out into the clearing. He slid down a tree and slumped to the ground, resting his face in the cup of his hands.

"C'mon, Wilkins, don't give up so fast," said Ken.

"Yeah," said Winston, "don't tell me I'm dressed up like a drag queen for nothing."

"Hey, here they come!" said Ken, spotting the group through the trees. They could hear the sounds of footsteps approaching as the girls wound their way back through the woods, chanting all the while.

Todd jumped up, his heart beating fast. "OK, guys, let's hide behind the tree and try to get one of the girls' attention as they come by."

"Maybe I can distract Jessica," said Ken.

"That might be hard," said Winston. "I think she's playing drill sergeant."

The boys crouched behind the tree, ready to pounce on the girls as they jogged by. Suddenly they heard the sounds of footsteps approaching from the clearing in the other direction.

They turned quickly. Walking toward them from a distance was Zoe Balsam flanked by two large men. They were all wearing the navy-blue director's uniforms of the American Cheerleading Association.

"Oh, no, it's the head of the ACA!" despaired Todd.

"And some flight attendants!" added Winston.

"C'mon, let's get out of here!" urged Ken, jumping up and heading away from the directors.

"Wait!" Todd said, reaching out and stopping him. "We've got to keep going in the same direction or else we'll look suspicious."

"You're right," Ken said, nodding. The three of them took off at a slow jog, trying to appear normal.

Todd's pulse quickened as they approached the directors.

"Hello!" Ken and Todd called out, waving as they passed. Winston managed a short wave and tripped along after them.

"Good morning, girls!" returned the directors, waving and smiling as they passed by.

Jessica headed to the bathroom to shower after the run, deep in thought. The girls were still out on the practice field, doing a series of cool-down exercises under Lila's guidance. Jessica wondered how they'd fare during the second round of the competition without Heather. They'd done a great job at the third competition the day before, but that hadn't been good enough. Today they had to be better than great. They had to be extraordinary.

The words of Jade Wu came back to her: *Without Heather we're ordinary. Without Heather we're ordinary.* The comment had been haunting her all night. Jessica had scorned the idea, but Jade's words weren't lost on her. Before Heather had arrived at Sweet Valley, the cheerleading squad had been good, but not outstanding. They'd never competed in the regional competition before, not to mention state—or nationals. When Heather had come along, she had turned the team around. Jessica wondered, deep down, if Jade was right. Maybe Heather *was* the key to their success.

Jessica pushed open the door to the bathroom and heard the sounds of somebody weeping.

"Hey, are you OK?" she asked, peeping under the stall to see who it was. "Oh, it's you," she said, making a face as she recognized Heather's custom-made cheerleading shoes. She went to the sink and turned on the faucet to wash her hands.

Jessica could hear Heather sniff and blow her nose. "Go ahead," Heather said in an obstinate tone through the door. "Tell me how I ruined everything. Tell me how I humiliated the entire squad. Tell me how you hate me."

Jessica turned off the water and leaned back against the sink. Heather's sob story wasn't going to work on her. Heather had dug her own grave, and Jessica refused to pity her for it.

"OK," she said as Heather emerged from the

stall. "You ruined everything. You humiliated the entire squad. I—"

"Oh, stop it," Heather growled, coming out of the stall and turning to the sink to wash her hands. "If it weren't for me, you wouldn't even be here in the first place."

Jessica could feel the blood rush to her face. "You've got a lot of nerve!" she cried. "How dare you take any credit when you've as much as ruined our chances at nationals? Why don't you just admit the truth, Heather? You may be a great cheerleader, but you just can't cut it in the big leagues."

Heather opened her mouth as if to respond but quickly checked herself.

"Go ahead," Jessica goaded her. "Admit it. You're not good enough. You can't take the pressure."

"That is not true!" Heather said between clenched teeth.

"Oh, yeah?" Jessica said. "Then how do you explain your disastrous performances on the field today?"

"I had no choice," Heather said quietly. "I had to do it."

"I knew it!" Jessica exclaimed. "You messed up on purpose. You were trying to humiliate me."

"Oh, Jessica," said Heather scornfully. "This doesn't have anything to do with you. Contrary to what you may believe, the world doesn't revolve around you."

"It doesn't?" Jessica said, surprised. "What do you mean?"

Heather sighed. "It's kind of a long story."

A few minutes later they were sitting on their bunks in the deserted cabin. "OK, let's have it," said Jessica.

"Well, remember the girl you met at lunch from my old squad?" Heather began, getting up and pacing the room as she spoke.

How could I forget? thought Jessica, thinking of the tall, beautiful brunette who had practically run her over on their first day there. "Marissa James," Jessica confirmed.

Heather nodded. "Well, she heard from everyone that Sweet Valley would be Thomas Jefferson's biggest rival at the nationals. So in typical Marissa James style she decided to stop us."

"What do you mean?" It had never occurred to Jessica that anybody else but Heather was responsible for their problems. "But how did she plan to do it?"

"By blackmailing me to mess up the competition," Heather confessed.

"Blackmailing you?" said Jessica, aghast. "With what?"

"With this!" said Heather, pulling out the article.

Just at that moment the door swung open. "Jessica Wakefield, I have something to say to you," said Elizabeth, stomping through the door with a vehement look on her face. All the girls piled in behind her.

"Wait, listen—" began Jessica.

"No, you listen to me for once," interrupted Elizabeth, the words coming out in a flood. "You

126

can't just push people around and get your own way all the time. You can't hold secret meetings and make important decisions without the input of all the members of the squad. We've been talking, and the whole team has agreed that it was unorthodox of you to vote without me. Your vote is officially null and void. If you want Heather off the squad, we *all* have to agree to it!"

Elizabeth stared at her sister, darts shooting from her eyes. The other girls shuffled nervously, waiting for a reprisal from Jessica.

"It's not necessary, Elizabeth," Heather said, slumping down on the bunk. "I've agreed not to be on the team."

"What are you talking about?" she asked, turning to face Heather.

"You had better tell them the whole story," Jessica said.

"What story?" Elizabeth asked.

Heather sighed. "I guess you should all hear this."

"Sounds juicy," Jessica heard Lila whisper to Amy as the two girls plopped down onto Lila's bunk. Jean, Maria, and Sandy piled onto Jean's bunk, leaning against the wood-slatted wall. The rest of the girls settled down on the floor in front of them.

When all eyes were turned toward Heather, she began to recount her tale.

"At TJ, I was the best cheerleader," Heather said. "I was the head of the squad, and I took our team to State for two years in a row."

Jessica sighed, then interrupted. "I think we've already heard all this before," she said.

"Do you mind?" asked Heather.

"OK, sorry. Go on," Jessica said.

Heather closed her eyes for a moment, as if to get hold of herself, and continued. "Well, it all happened around this time last year," she said. "We had just won at State, and we were preparing for nationals. Cheerleading was my life. It was all that mattered to me. I devoted so much time to cheerleading that my grades began to slide. Especially my math grade. The final exam was coming up, and I knew that I was going to fail. And if I failed, I would be kicked off the squad."

"So you cheated on the final," guessed Sandy.

"And you were kicked off the squad," added Jean.

"Right." Heather nodded.

"How did you manage to cheat on the test?" Amy asked.

"I, uh, got a copy of the exam before the final," Heather explained, bright-pink circles popping out on her cheeks. "And to make things even worse, I gave it to a few of my friends. That was how I got caught. We all had the same answers, and they weren't all right."

"How awful!" Annie exclaimed.

"Yeah, it was a big scandal, and my reputation at school was ruined. And in the entire town." She waved the article in the air as proof.

"Let's see," said Lila, stretching a hand out for the story. Lila skimmed it quickly and passed it on.

The girls murmured sympathetically as they read the incriminating account.

"But, Heather, we don't care about all that," said Annie, passing the story on to Maria. "You've already been punished as it is."

"Yeah, that's all in the past now," said Sara.

"Not exactly," said Heather. "You see, the first night at nationals, I found the article in my bed—planted by Marissa James."

The girls murmured in surprise.

"Marissa was my archenemy at TJ," explained Heather. "She wanted to be the captain for two years in a row, and the girls voted for me both years. So, anyway, Marissa told me that if I let Sweet Valley so much as *place* in a single competition, my secret would be out."

"She blackmailed you!" exclaimed Sara.

"That is despicable!" said Annie angrily. "That girl should be kicked out of the ACA."

"Well, it doesn't matter now," said Heather, her lips suddenly trembling as she spoke. "You know, when I came to Sweet Valley, I thought I'd have the chance to start over again. I thought I'd have a new beginning. But it looks like my past is destined to follow me around for the rest of my life."

"No, it's not!" objected Annie.

"That's ridiculous!" chimed in Sara. Jessica rolled her eyes. She couldn't believe how sympathetically the girls were responding. *You'd think that now at least they'd see Heather for what she really is,* she thought.

"You can still start over!" said Jean encouragingly.

"No, I can't," said Heather, shaking her head, "because I've ruined everything. I shouldn't have gone along with Marissa's scheme. I just couldn't bear the thought of my secret coming out." Tears trickled down her cheeks as she spoke. "I realize now that I should have told you all right away. I— I'm truly sorry. Now I hate myself, probably more than all of you hate me now."

"Why, Heather, that would be impossible," Jessica started to say, but she was interrupted by Patty Gilbert, who stood up and took the floor. Patty had been sitting with a pencil and paper during Heather's confession.

"Each round of the competition is worth one third of the total score, right?" said Patty. The girls nodded their heads. "And right now, we're thirty-fifth. It doesn't look like we can win. But if we come in first in all the competitions from now on, we can still place."

"Well, then," said Elizabeth. "Enough of this sitting around. Let's get out of here!"

"Wow, what a story!" said Lila, whistling under her breath. She and Jessica were walking to the field for the first competition of the day.

"I know," said Jessica. "The whole time I thought she was out to get me. And it turned out that Marissa James was out to get her." Jessica shook her head in wonder. "I never dreamed that somebody else was involved."

"You know, I almost feel sorry for her," said Lila.

130

"Well, I don't!" said Jessica emphatically. She ducked under a tree branch jutting out in the path. "I mean, it's too bad that she got kicked off her squad and suffered complete and utter humiliation." Jessica paused to savor the thought of it. "But that doesn't negate her heinous behavior the whole time she's been on the squad. And she should have told us right away about the black-mailing thing."

"I think the team feels pretty sympathetic toward her," said Lila. A fly buzzed noisily around her face, and she swatted it away.

"Wonders never cease," said Jessica. "I swear, that girl could rob them all and they'd thank her."

"Well, I think we should thank her for telling us the truth," said Lila. "I mean, when you're in that deep, it's hard to get out. Now we've still got a chance."

"Yeah," agreed Jessica, "we'll show Marissa James that Sweet Valley High can't be pushed around!"

Just then Marissa James approached them on the walk, looking fit and fashionable in a black Lycra unitard. Dark sunglasses were propped up on her head, holding back a thatch of rich auburn hair.

"Speak of the devil," Lila muttered under her breath.

"The devil is right," Jessica agreed.

"Oh, hi," Marissa said as she caught sight of them.

"Hi," Jessica and Lila returned, waving back unenthusiastically.

"So sorry you've all had such a rough time of it," she said as she passed, her voice dripping with false sympathy. "Oh, well, maybe next year!" she called.

"Or maybe *this* year," muttered Lila.

"I really hate that girl," said Jessica.

Chapter 10

"R-O-W-D-I-E, that's the way we spell row-die!" yelled Jessica, stamping her feet energetically as the squad launched into their standard school-spirit routine.

"Rowdie, let's get rowdie!" sang out the girls, hitting their hands against their thighs and stomping their feet in unison to the beat. It was the first competition of the day, and the Sweet Valley squad was performing brilliantly. The crowd was on its feet, clapping and stomping along with the music.

Jessica was beaming as she and Heather led the squad into the final leg of the routine. It was a jazzy dance number that Jade and Patty had choreographed. Clapping and shouting, the girls formed two lines facing each other, Jessica and Heather heading each row.

As the music shifted to an upbeat tempo, the girls sprang into action. Working in pairs, the girls did one-armed cartwheels toward each other in perfect succession. They followed with a line of front handsprings. As Heather and Jessica bounced back onto their heels, Jade and Patty performed a back crunch: a round-off followed by a back handspring. The other pairs quickly followed.

The last stunt was a front handspring followed by a spread-eagle jump with a landing in the splits. Heather and Jessica landed next to each other, and the other girls fanned out, forming a perfect V. "V-I-C-T-O-R-Y, that's Sweet Valley's battle cry!" they yelled, holding their arms up in the air in V shapes.

The audience applauded wildly, rising spontaneously to their feet.

Static filled the air, and a voice came over the loudspeaker. "Everybody please settle down," boomed the announcer. "Our last squad has performed. We'll have the results in just a moment."

The girls trotted off the field, out of breath but elated at the response to their performance.

"We did it!" said Jean as they took their seats in the bleachers.

"We were definitely not ordinary!" agreed Jade, laughing.

"The third-place winner in the first round of today's competition is the squad from Reno, Nevada!" boomed the announcer.

Jessica gritted her teeth as the Reno squad stood up and yelled out a cheer. Marissa's voice rang out loud and clear across the stadium as she led them in their school-spirit cheer. "Now we've really got to win," said Jessica to Lila, her voice determined.

The announcer's voice came over the loudspeaker again. "And the second-place prize goes to our most exotic squad—the Waikiki Pelicans all the way from Waikiki, Hawaii!"

Jessica grabbed on to Lila's hand for support as the audience applauded. This was their only chance. If they didn't win now, they were out of the competition for good.

"Jess!" Lila said, wriggling her hand. Jessica looked down. She was gripping Lila's hand so hard that her knuckles were turning white.

"Oh, sorry," she said, loosening her grip. Jessica closed her eyes and held her breath as the announcer continued.

"And our first-place winners—shocking us all with their amazing turnaround—the squad from Sweet Valley, California!" boomed the announcer.

The girls exploded with joy, hugging and high-fiving each other. Jessica glanced over at Heather. Heather looked back at her and winked. Jessica smiled. It looked as if everything was going to be OK after all.

"Do you think I could talk to you for a moment?" said Marissa James, yanking Heather away from the squad as the girls headed to lunch at the lodge.

"Sure," said Heather sweetly, pulling her arm away and stepping away from the group.

Marissa waited until the girls were out of earshot.

"Have you forgotten our little agreement?" she hissed. Her even features were contorted with rage, and she looked as if she were about to explode.

"No, Marissa, I haven't forgotten," said Heather evenly. "I've just decided it doesn't matter."

Marissa stared at her in astonishment.

"You see, I told my squad about the old Heather Mallone myself," Heather explained. "There's nothing you can say about me that they don't already know. Now you'll have to compete against the Sweet Valley squad in all their strength."

"You'll never win, you little weasel," Marissa snarled. "And I'll do everything in my power to make sure about that."

"I wouldn't waste my energy on our squad if I were you," Heather returned. "You'll need all of it for your own." Heather flipped her blond mane over her shoulders and walked calmly away.

"Are we all set?" Jessica asked on Sunday afternoon at the cabin as the girls got ready to leave for the second competition of the day. The event was scheduled to begin in half an hour, and the Braselton girls had already left for the field.

Jessica looked around at her squad proudly. They were dressed in Heather's tailor-made uniforms for their seventies disco routine. Both Heather and Jessica had agreed to wear Lila's uniforms for the grand finale. The girls were all decked out in red-and-white-checked hip-hugging skirts and half tops. Jessica had to admit they looked sharp.

"Ready to boogie down!" said Jeanie.

"Do the hustle!" sang Sandy. Everybody laughed as Jeanie and Sandy broke out into an exaggerated version of the dance. The girls were all pumped up from their victory in the morning, and they were ready to bring the house down again.

"Jean, you've got the pom-poms?" Jessica asked.

"Got 'em," said Jean, holding up the pom-pom bag.

"And Lila, you're bringing the routine book?" Jessica asked. Lila held it up in confirmation.

"I've got the music," offered Heather.

"OK, then!" Jessica said. She drew the girls toward her for a group hug. "Let's go get 'em!" she yelled. The girls clapped and let out a whoop.

Jessica slung her backpack over her back and bounced up to the door. She put her hand on the knob and pulled. It seemed to be stuck. "Wha—?" she said out loud, turning the knob and tugging at the door. It didn't budge. "I can't seem to get the door open," Jessica said.

"Let me try," Heather said, closing her hand firmly over the knob and pulling with all her might. The door wheezed in protest but didn't move. Heather took a deep breath and tried again, exerting all her force. Nothing. "How could the door be locked?" Heather asked, perplexed.

Jessica and Heather stared at each other in wonder, and then suddenly it dawned on them at the same time. "Marissa James," they said in unison.

Jessica turned and faced the girls. "It looks like Marissa James and her squad have been up to some mischief," she said. "The door's locked from the outside."

"And we're stuck in here," Heather added.

"Oh, no!" said Maria in despair, falling back onto a bunk.

"What are we going to do?" wailed Sandy.

"I don't know," said Heather, looking at her watch. "Our performance starts in half an hour. If we don't get to the field in time, we'll be automatically disqualified from the entire competition."

Jessica marched up to the door and yanked at it violently, a fierce expression on her face. The door stood firm. "Darnit!" Jessica cried, slamming her fist into the hard wood. It took her a moment to register the pain. "Owwl!" she moaned, hopping around holding her hand.

"Jessica, are you OK?" asked Annie with concern, jumping up and running toward her.

"I'm fine, I'm fine," said Jessica, waving her away.

"Let's try the windows," Heather suggested, indicating the four windows lining the cabin walls. She quickly turned the handle of one of the windows and pulled. It didn't move. She braced her legs against the wall and yanked again, putting her whole body into it. Suddenly she went flying back across the room and fell onto a bunk, the handle in her hand. "Well, that one's out of the question," Heather said wryly, dropping the handle to the floor with a clatter.

The girls quickly made a circuit of the cabin, trying all the windows in succession, but their efforts were in vain. The windows were all sealed shut.

"I can't believe it," Heather muttered angrily, perching on the corner of a bunk. She stared at her watch, watching as the minutes ticked away. "All our work—"

"And now we don't even have a chance!" finished Annie.

"We're doomed," despaired Jean, dropping the bag of pom-poms onto the floor and slumping down on the ground.

"There must be *some* way we can get out of here," Jessica said in determination, looking around the wooden cabin frantically in search of an exit. She felt as if the wooden walls were closing in her. *Maybe they could break down the door,* she thought desperately. This was their only chance for a comeback. If they didn't compete now, her reputation as cocaptain was ruined. Suddenly her eyes lit upon the tiny window high on the wall at the back of the cabin. A crack of light shone through it. "That one's open!" Jessica exclaimed. All the girls followed her gaze.

"Jessica, are you crazy?" said Lila in wonder. "It's about two feet square."

"I bet Jade could get through it," said Jessica, indicating the slight, petite girl.

Jade looked nervous. "But it must be over twenty feet up," she said. "We'd need a ladder."

"Well, we're a cheerleading squad, aren't we?" said Jessica enthusiastically. "We make our own ladders!"

"Jessica's right!" enthused Heather. "We'll make a pyramid!" She stopped and thought for a moment, quickly measuring the space from the floor to the ceiling in her head. "I think we're going to have to do a four-three-two-one pyramid."

"A four-tiered pyramid!" breathed Elizabeth.

"Is that possible?" asked Sara.

"Usually not," admitted Heather. "But I think it's worth a try."

"Yeah, what have we got to lose?" added Jessica.

"Our lives, for one thing," said Elizabeth dryly.

"It is kind of dangerous," Heather agreed.

"So Heather and I will spot the pyramid on either side," Jessica said.

Heather nodded her head in agreement.

"Let's get moving, then!" said Lila, jumping up. "We've only got about fifteen minutes left."

"OK," said Jessica, surveying the squad, "biggest girls on the bottom and smallest on top." She quickly assigned positions. Patty, Lila, Amy, and Sara got down on the floor on all fours. Maria, Annie, and Elizabeth assumed their positions on top of them quickly, making the second tier.

"Everybody close in for support," said Heather. The girls shifted together, forming a tight fit. Jessica and Heather spotted Jean and Sandy as they climbed up the tiers. The pyramid swayed dangerously as they settled on top. Jessica and Heather quickly flanked the sides, holding the girls together. "Deep breath, everyone," said Jessica. "Steady!"

"Well, here goes," Jade said, biting her lip nervously.

Heather crouched down as Jade climbed onto her shoulders. Moving adeptly, Jade supported her full weight with her arms and swung her dancer's legs up onto Heather's shoulders. She stood and balanced carefully. Holding on to the ceiling for support, Jade placed her knees delicately on the third tier of the pyramid, careful to distribute her weight between Jean and Sandy equally. The girls held their breath as Jade released her hold on Heather. The pyramid stood.

"OK, guys," said Jessica in a soothing voice, "you look great. Now, just stay calm."

Jade reached up to the window carefully. Her fingers barely grazed the handle. She took a deep breath and stretched out on her knees, grabbing hold of the handle firmly. A triumphant grin spread across her face as she pulled the window open entirely.

"Heads up!" Sandy yelled as she felt the pyramid collapsing. Jade's hand slipped from the handle as her support began to give way. Jessica and Heather jumped to the sides, protecting the girls from the bunks as they slid down into a pile on the ground.

"Well, we did it," said Jade, peeking her head out from the mass of arms and legs. "We made a four-three-two-one pyramid."

The girls groaned and lay back in a heap on the floor.

✿   ✿   ✿

"I've never seen so many cheerleaders in my entire life!" exclaimed Todd as he took in the scene before him. Todd, Ken, and Winston were seated at the far end of the bleachers, waiting for the second competition to begin. The field was bursting with groups of enthusiastic girls cheering and shouting as they practiced their routines. With all the squads in matching uniforms, the field had been transformed into a rainbow of colors.

"Me neither," Ken agreed. "Can you imagine having this many girls cheer you on at a game?"

"We'd win every point," said Todd.

"Girls, please take your seats!" yelled a voice over the loudspeakers. "The competition is about to begin!"

Todd, Ken, and Winston clustered together trying to look inconspicuous as the girls began filling the stands.

"Where do you think they are?" Todd asked, glancing down at his watch nervously. "The competition starts in five minutes." Todd looked over at the empty California section of the stands, a worried expression on his face.

"Every other team is here," said Ken, taking in the packed stands. Most of the squads were huddled together, giving pep talks and letting out small cheers.

"Don't worry, they'll be here," Winston reassured them. "They're probably doing warm-up exercises in the practice field."

"Unless they've passed out from their run this morning," said Todd.

142

"Well, you know Jessica," said Ken. "She wouldn't miss the competition for anything in the world. She's probably planning to make a grand entrance."

"She could be late, though," worried Todd. "Jessica doesn't wear a watch."

"But Elizabeth does," Ken pointed out.

"Please give a warm welcome to the Texas Tigers from San Antonio, Texas, our first squad to perform!" boomed the voice over the loudspeaker. The crowd clapped as a group of spirited girls in orange-and-black outfits bounced onto the field.

"They're starting!" Ken exclaimed in surprise.

Winston leafed through the program quickly, running a finger down the day's lineup. "Sweet Valley is the fifth team to perform in this competition."

"That gives the girls about ten minutes," said Todd. "We better go find them." The boys jumped up and tore down the bleachers, taking the steps two at a time.

"Why is everybody looking at us?" Todd asked as they trotted across the field, noting the funny looks they were drawing from the crowd. As they passed each squad, the cheerleaders seemed to gather together in groups, laughing and pointing.

"Don't worry about it, Todd," said Ken, holding on to his skirt as he ran. "We're popular, that's all."

"Whoa, mama!" yelled a girl from the audience, putting her fingers in her mouth and letting out a piercing whistle.

"Show us some leg!" hooted another girl.

143

"Oh, boy," moaned Winston, limping along after Ken and Todd. "I think they know who we are."

"Hey! Someone's coming!" Lila said, looking out the side window from her bunk. "Three cheerleaders. Three really funny-looking cheerleaders."

"Are they coming for us?" asked Maria.

"I hope so," said Lila.

The girls all piled onto Lila's bunk, shouting and waving out the window. "Help, help!" they yelled. "We're in here!"

"Let me see," said Jessica, trying to get a glimpse out the window. "Wow," she said. "The Amazon queens are coming."

Jessica leaned back against the wall, the relief evident on her face. "I can't believe it," she said. "We might make it to the competition after all."

Maria clambered up to the window, watching as two huge cheerleaders and one tall, skinny cheerleader lumbered toward the cabin. As she watched, the tall, skinny cheerleader's hair fell off. Maria gasped in shock.

"Oh-mi-god!" she screamed a moment later as Winston ran back to retrieve his wig. "It's Winston!" She waved a hand toward the others to look.

"And that's Ken and Todd!" Amy exclaimed.

Maria jumped off the bunk and ran to the door. She began knocking on it loudly, trying to get the boys' attention. Soon all of the girls had crowded around her. "Help, help!" they cried, pounding on the door as the boys approached.

"Don't worry, we're coming!" yelled Todd.

"Help is on the way!" added Ken, quickly unlocking the door and pushing it open. A throng of girls almost fell on top of them.

"Oh, hi, girls," said Ken with a smile, finding himself in a sea of cheerleaders.

"We might say the same thing!" exclaimed Maria as she took in the boys' lavishly made-up faces and cheerleading costumes.

All the girls started laughing as they got a glimpse of their liberators close-up.

"Where are you girls from?" asked Maria, noting the *S* on the boys' sweaters.

"Saskatchewan," Todd and Ken answered in unison.

"Saskatchewan!" responded Jeanie. "You came all the way from Canada!"

"I hear they're known for their husky cheerleaders," said Sandy.

"They've got some *sizable* talent there, don't they?" added Maria.

Maria's pun sent the girls into fresh gales of laughter. Everybody was laughing uproariously—except Jessica and Elizabeth, Maria noticed. They had both backed away from the group and were sitting on opposite bunks at the far end of the cabin. Obviously cheerleading costumes hadn't done the trick.

"All right, all right, that's enough," said Todd.

"Everybody up," said Ken. "You've got a performance to put on."

"I think the performance is already taking place," said Sandy merrily.

The girls stood up and gathered their bags, wiping away tears of laughter from their eyes.

"You know, Winston," said Maria, entwining her elbow in his and cuddling up to him. "I always did have a thing for redheads."

"You know what they say about us," said Winston with a goofy grin, hugging her closer to him and leaning down for a kiss. "We're fiery and passionate." Maria smiled as she wiped the lipstick from her lips.

"And hotheaded," added Sandy. "Maria, you better watch out."

"I think I'll take my chances," said Maria with a smile.

"Ken, who does your hair?" breathed Lila, sidling up to him. "That blond do is perfect with your eyes."

"Antonio," said Ken with mock seriousness. "But he's very expensive."

"Hey, Todd, want to borrow my lipstick?" asked Amy, holding out a bright-colored tube.

"Now, cut it out, you guys!" Todd said, shaking a pom-pom at all of them. "You have about a minute and a half to get onstage!"

Chapter 11

"And for the second time in a row, the number-one squad is Sweet Valley High!" boomed the announcer's voice over the loudspeaker system following the afternoon competition.

The crowd applauded enthusiastically as the band struck up a lively tune. The girls from the Sweet Valley squad went wild, jumping up and down with joy and throwing pom-poms in the air.

Jessica's knees buckled with relief, and she sat down hard on the bleachers. After all the excitement she suddenly felt drained. The girls had arrived on the field with about fifteen seconds to spare. They hadn't even had time for a pep talk. They had run straight onto the field and started their number. But they had been so pumped up with nervous energy that they had performed more brilliantly than ever.

"We did it!" yelled Sandy, grabbing Jeanie and flinging her around.

147

"We really pulled it off!" said Maria. "C'mon, Jess!" she said, grabbing Jessica by the hands and pulling her up. Jessica found herself caught up in a whirlwind of girls hugging and congratulating each other. Suddenly she felt herself being swung around by Heather.

As soon as Heather realized it was Jessica, she let go of her grip. Jessica and Heather looked at each other awkwardly for a moment, then shrugged and moved away. *Who would have ever thought I'd be hugging Heather?* pondered Jessica, shaking her head in amazement.

"The crowd went nuts over the disco stuff," said Maria as the girls began settling down.

"Yeah, and that jump by Heather really brought down the house!" said Annie. Jessica rankled at Annie's words. Heather, as usual, had virtually taken over the performance with her flashy dance-jump combination at the end of the routine. But it *had* been amazing, she had to admit.

"And we owe it all to the boys!" said Maria.

"Or the girls!" said Annie.

"They're getting more attention than anyone else here," said Jeanie.

"Well, of course they are," said Sandy. "Three boys in the midst of an all-girls event—what would you expect?"

"Yeah, all the girls are thrilled," said Lila.

"But the judges wouldn't be if they knew," said Maria. "I don't think the directors have caught on yet either."

"Lucky for us," put in Amy. "The boys really

saved us today. I thought it was all over."

"Let's go thank them," said Maria, slinging her bag over her shoulder and jumping up.

"Uh, I've got some stuff to take care of at the cabin," said Elizabeth quickly, hopping up and sprinting down the bleachers.

"Me too," Jessica said, taking off after her sister.

Amy and Maria looked at each other after the twins made their rapid exit.

"Something's got to be done about this," Maria said.

"Yeah," agreed Amy. "This is getting unbearable. We've got to get the twins back together—with each other and with their boyfriends."

"Let's go find the boys—I mean, the girls," suggested Maria.

Maria scanned the athletic field quickly. "I think they're over there, hiding from the crowds," she said, pointing across the field. Sure enough, the boys were huddled together at the far end of the field, trying to keep a low profile as hordes of cheerleaders streamed by them.

Amy and Maria ran down the bleachers and made their way across the field.

Maria couldn't help laughing as she took in Winston's attire. Her heart went out to him with love. With his long, skinny limbs and knobby knees, Winston always looked a little goofy. In his cheerleading outfit he looked ridiculous, like a bony stork dressed in a skirt.

Maria ran up to him and jumped into his arms.

Winston quickly unraveled himself, a horrified

expression on his face. "No public displays of affection as long as I'm a woman!" he said.

Maria clapped her hand to her mouth. "That's right!" she said, laughing. "What would the judges think!"

"You could be disqualified for intersquad affection," said Ken.

"Well, in your fancy outfits you *are* pretty hard to resist," said Maria.

"Yeah, what's with the plumage, Winston?" asked Amy.

"Are you going to the Oscars after this?" teased Maria.

"Well, you know, I really wanted to make a splash," said Winston.

"He thought he should go all out for Maria," added Todd.

"You're welcome to borrow *my* outfit sometime," said Ken, speaking in a high-pitched tone. He paused a moment to pose, putting a hand to his hair and shaking his blond curls. "But only if I can borrow yours. I love hip huggers."

"Oh, Ken, you're so lucky," said Todd in a high voice. "With my hips I'd never get away with it."

Everybody laughed.

Suddenly Todd turned serious as he noticed the rest of the Sweet Valley High cheerleaders making their way down the bleachers. "Hey, you guys, they're leaving!" Todd said. "We've got to catch up with Jessica and Elizabeth." Todd shaded his eyes with his hand as he tried to pick them out.

"Bad news, Todd," said Maria. "They already left."

"Bolted is more like it," Amy added.

Todd's face fell.

"Do you think it was the skirt?" Ken asked.

"Listen, you guys," said Amy. "You've got to get those two talking again."

"And get back together with them," added Maria. "They've been at each other's throats!"

Elizabeth walked through the woods alone on her way back to the cabin, laughing as she remembered how cute Todd looked in his little pleated skirt. She hugged her arms around herself, feeling a flood of warmth as she thought of Todd. The sun was shining brightly and the sky was a clear robin's-egg blue. A hummingbird whirred from a branch nearby. Elizabeth almost felt happy for a moment.

Then she remembered that she and Todd were broken up, and her high spirits evaporated instantly into the crisp afternoon air. Todd was no longer hers. She couldn't carry him around with her in her thoughts any longer. She couldn't dream of him anymore. She couldn't look forward to seeing him, to talking with him, laughing with him, lying in his arms. . . .

Why did he have to come here? Elizabeth thought in frustration, kicking at a pebble in the path. It was bad enough being broken up with him. Seeing him only made things worse. She wondered what he was doing there. He obviously hadn't come to see her. Todd had made it crystal clear that he wouldn't have anything to do with her. The pain of their conversation stung her again. Todd would never forgive her. And deservedly so, Elizabeth thought, hanging her head. She had betrayed his trust—and his love—with his best friend.

So what is he doing here? she wondered again. Maybe Ken wanted to make up with Jessica, and he had talked Todd into coming along. That was it, Elizabeth decided. Todd was trying to help out his best friend.

Well, Elizabeth thought sadly as she trudged up the hill to the cabin, *at least Ken and Todd are friends again.*

"I have no idea why Ken bothered to come all the way to Yosemite dressed like a transvestite," declared Jessica, "because I'm never going to have anything to do with him."

"Jessica, sometimes you can be so stubborn," Lila said, tucking a loose strand of hair behind her ear.

Jessica and Lila were sharing a banana split at the Crystal Ice Palace, an ice-cream parlor down the road from the cheerleading compound. They had sneaked away after the competition to get away from the gang.

"I am not being stubborn," said Jessica. She picked a maraschino cherry out of the whipped cream and popped it into her mouth. "I'm being completely reasonable."

Lila lifted a heaping spoonful of strawberry ice cream and hot fudge to her mouth. "Mpphh thnk mmpph formmmm mmph."

"What?" Jessica asked, cutting into a sliced banana with a spoon.

Lila dabbed her mouth with her napkin. "I said, I think you should forgive him."

"I thought that's what you said," said Jessica with a sigh. "I just can't imagine *why* you said it." Jessica speared the banana wedge with her knife and swirled it in the dish, smothering it with ice cream and hot fudge. Leaning over the dish, she popped her creation into her mouth. "Mmm!" she said, licking her lips. "This is yummy!"

"It ain't Casey's, but it'll do," said Lila. Casey's Ice Cream Parlor was a popular spot for dessert at the Valley Mall. It was Lila and Jessica's favorite place to take a break after a hard day of shopping.

Jessica wiped her mouth and leaned back in her chair, feeling dizzy from the ice cream she had just inhaled. "Here, you have the rest," she said, pushing the dish away from her.

"Thanks," Lila said, dipping a finger into the whipped cream.

"So, anyway," Jessica said. "You were trying to convince me to forgive Ken."

"You know, Jess, he didn't really do anything," Lila said.

"Yes, he did," insisted Jessica. "He went out on a date with my sister—a romantic date at the beach— *our* beach. And then he kissed her." Jessica shivered at the thought.

"But Jessica, he thought he was kissing you," said Lila.

"Exactly," said Jessica, putting her finger in the air. "Obviously I don't stand out." She leaned forward in her chair. "It's like that game show—*Kiss and Tell*—where the contestants have to guess who their partners are from a kiss." Jessica sat back in her chair, folding her hands together on her lap as if she had just made a brilliant point. "If Ken and I went on the show, he would get the consolation prize—a plastic pair of big red lips."

Lila rolled her eyes. "Fortunately for you, this isn't *Kiss and Tell*. It's real life."

Jessica shrugged her shoulders. "That's not the point. The point is that he couldn't distinguish between me and my sister—*in real life*," she said, emphasizing the last three words.

"Jessica, he realized immediately that he was kissing Elizabeth," Lila said, taking another stab at it. "And then he came to tell you right away." Lila brought a spoonful of chocolate ice cream and whipped cream to her mouth and pushed the ice cream to the middle of the table.

"Ken didn't tell me anything," Jessica said. "Elizabeth told me the whole sordid story."

"But that's because you wouldn't speak to him," Lila pointed out.

"Hmmph!" said Jessica stubbornly. "I don't care if he tried to tell me about it or not. If Ken can't distinguish me from my sister, then he must not really love me."

Lila waved a perfectly manicured hand in the air. "Fine, I give up," she said. She sat back and took a long drink of ice water.

154

"Good," said Jessica. But inside Jessica wondered if Lila was right. She missed Ken desperately. She wanted to be able to forgive him. But there was no way she was going to let him know it, she resolved, digging into the ice cream with a renewed fury.

Chapter 12

"OK, Liz, don't move," said Maria, sitting behind Elizabeth on her bunk as she twisted Elizabeth's hair into a French braid.

"Shoot!" Maria muttered as the silky strands slipped out of her hand. She unwound them and brushed out Elizabeth's thick hair again, separating it adroitly into three strands. Starting from the crown, she began weaving her hair into shiny golden-blond plaits.

Elizabeth sat perfectly still as she took in the commotion around her. The girls were all wearing red unitards as they got ready for the third competition, and it was like a circus in the cabin. The Alabama squad had already left for the field. As usual, the Sweet Valley squad was running a little late. The atmosphere was a bit frenetic, with girls running around frantically trying to get ready in time for the competition.

"Hey, Sandy, have you seen my lipstick?" asked Jean, sitting cross-legged on her bunk with a compact open in front of her.

"Here, use this," Sandy responded, sorting through her cosmetic bag. She tossed a tube through the air.

"Thanks," Jean said, catching the lipstick adeptly in one hand. She pursed her lips into a cupid bow and deftly outlined her mouth.

"Jessica, can I use the blow-dryer when you're done?" asked Sara, tapping Jessica on the shoulder. Jessica was bent over, drying her hair upside down. Her blond hair fell in a curtain around her face.

"What?" Jessica asked, straightening up and shutting off the dryer.

"I said, can I use the blow-dryer when you're done?" Sara repeated.

"Oh, sure," Jessica said, flipping her hair upside down and fluffing it around her face. Her cheeks were flushed a rosy pink from the heat, and her eyes sparkled brightly. Jessica smiled into the mirror on the wall, pleased with the effect. "Here, I think I'm done." She handed the blow-dryer to Sara.

Amy was rummaging around in the squad duffel bag, fishing for a medium-sized cheerleading costume.

"Hey, Amy, can you get one for me, too?" Lila asked, meticulously plucking her eyebrows. She carefully tweezed her left eyebrow into a thin, arched line.

"Sure," said Amy. She pulled out two red-and-white costumes and threw one to Lila. Lila swiped it out of the air with one hand and hopped up from the bunk.

"OK, girls," Jessica said, "five more minutes and we're out of here!"

Lila and Amy quickly pulled on their skirts.

"Oh-mi-god," said Amy, staring at the skirt lying in a heap around her feet.

"What the—?" muttered Lila as her skirt slipped to the floor.

All the commotion came to a sudden halt as the girls gathered around.

"Have you guys lost a lot of weight?" asked Sara.

"Let me see," said Maria, quickly pulling on a skirt. It dropped immediately to the floor. Maria kicked it up off the floor and examined it. "It's the elastic," she said. "It's missing."

One by one the girls tried on their skirts and watched as they fell to the floor. The elastic had been cut out of all of them.

"Looks like Marissa and her squad have struck," said Jessica grimly.

"Again," said Heather.

Jessica checked the door suddenly. It opened easily. "Well, we're not locked in this time," she said.

"We can get out, but we don't have anything to wear," said Sandy with a sigh, sliding down the wall dramatically and plopping down onto the pile of waistless skirts.

The girls were in a total panic.

"What are we going to do?" wailed Annie.

"Now we won't be able to compete!" despaired Jeanie.

"We can't let them get the best of us," determined Sara.

Soon all the girls were talking at once, complaining and throwing out suggestions.

"OK," said Jessica, taking charge. "Time for a squad powwow." All the girls piled onto her bed.

"Now, we've got three different uniforms left to wear," said Jessica. "Our standard SVH uniforms, the hip huggers, and our special outfits for the grand finale tomorrow."

"We can't wear the hip huggers again," said Heather. "I dropped them off at the lodge to be laundered this afternoon."

"What if we wore our outfits for tomorrow?" suggested Jade.

"Oh, that would be such a shame," said Patty. "We chose them especially for the grand finale."

"We can't wear them anyway," Jessica said, shaking her head. "They're locked away in the bus. We'd never get there in time."

The girls sat in silence for a moment, pondering the possibilities. They could hear the seconds slipping away with the quiet *tick tick tick* of Elizabeth's watch.

Suddenly Elizabeth jumped up. "I've got it!" she exclaimed. "The solution was in front of our noses the whole time."

"What?" asked Maria excitedly.

"We don't need those silly little skirts, anyway," Elizabeth said, always practical. "We're all

159

wearing catsuits, right? Let's just cheer in those!"

"Y'all really did a bang-up job out there!" Wilhemina enthused after the final competition of the day. The Sweet Valley High squad had placed first for the third time in a row, and the Alabama girls were accompanying Jessica and Elizabeth to the lodge for dinner.

Elizabeth smiled graciously. "Thanks," she said.

"You sure are makin' a comeback," said Peggy May admiringly. "Why, I plum thought you'd drop out after the first two competitions."

"We thought we might drop out too," Elizabeth said.

"Y'all really knocked 'em dead in those sexy outfits!" exclaimed Wilhemina.

"I think it was that twin bit that really swayed the judges," put in Peggy May. "Why, that mirror routine was so darn real that I had to keep looking twice to make sure there were really two of you."

"Y'all looked like sheer angels," added Wilhemina.

Elizabeth smiled at the term. She and Jessica weren't exactly acting like angels these days. But she had to agree with the Alabama girls. The performance had climaxed with a mirror-image routine by Jessica and Elizabeth. Gesturing like mimes, the twins had faced one another and moved in sync, acting as if they were looking into a mirror. The crowd had gone mad with delight as the twins perfectly mirrored each other's steps, gestures, and jumps.

"I think it's the Reno squad you've really got to watch out for now," Wilhemina babbled on.

"Yeah, those girls have been on your tail all day," added Peggy May.

"I think you're right," agreed Elizabeth. "They're still ranked first overall."

Elizabeth noticed Jessica's jaw clench. She expected her to comment, but Jessica remained conspicuously quiet. She was clearly still giving Elizabeth the silent treatment. The rest of the squad had split immediately following the competition in an obvious effort to force the girls together. For once Elizabeth was thankful for the chatter of the Alabama girls so she didn't have to walk in silence with Jessica all the way to the lodge.

As they rounded the bend, Elizabeth noticed Ken, Todd, and Winston waving to them from afar, decked out in their cheerleading uniforms. In spite of herself, Elizabeth's heart did a little trojan crunch at the sight of Todd. The boys were gesturing wildly, signaling for them to come over. Elizabeth couldn't bear the thought of facing Todd or of watching Ken attempt to win Jessica over. The color high in her cheeks, she carefully averted her gaze, as did Jessica.

But the boys' attempts hadn't gotten past the Alabama girls. "Darlin's, looks like those big girls over there are trying to get y'all's attention," said Wilhemina.

Jessica and Elizabeth looked over at Ken and Todd gesturing frantically from the top of the hill. They both waved back casually and kept on walking.

"What squad are those girls on?" Peggy May asked. "They sure are hearty lookin'."

Jessica and Elizabeth looked back and noticed the boys running after them. Winston's skirt kept flying up, revealing a pair of gangly, muscular legs. He was trying desperately to hold it down as he ran. Suddenly he tripped over a loose shoelace and clutched at Ken and Todd for support, causing all three of them to tumble to the ground.

Not being able to contain themselves any longer, Jessica and Elizabeth burst out laughing. "Oh-mi-god!" Jessica cried, tears running down her face. "Did you see Win—" Elizabeth gasped. "He—" They were laughing so hard they had to stop walking.

The Alabama girls stopped and stared at the twins in confusion. "Why, whatever is the matter?" asked one of the girls.

"Nothing, nothing," said Elizabeth, making a superhuman effort to control her laughter. "Those, uh, girls just took a tumble, that's all."

Jessica waved the girls away. "Go on ahead without us," she said. "We'll just be a minute."

As soon as the Alabama girls were out of sight, Jessica and Elizabeth burst out laughing again.

"I have never—" gasped Elizabeth with laughter, barely able to get the words out, "seen anything—so ludicrous—in my whole life—!"

"Did you see Winston?" asked Jessica, choking back her laughter.

"He looked like a bird with his skirt flapping in

the air!" Elizabeth burst out, fluttering her hands like wings. "He was ready to soar away!"

"And then he flew right into the boys!" exclaimed Jessica. "And they all went down."

Elizabeth nodded. "It was a crash landing," she said solemnly, sending Jessica into fresh peals of laughter.

Elizabeth couldn't resist taking another peek at the boys. Winston was crouched down with his skirt flying around his waist, trying to tie his shoelace. Todd was standing up, wiping the dirt off his knees. Ken was darting along the ground chasing after his wig, which had gotten caught in a gust of wind.

"Oh, oh!" cried Jessica, holding on to her stomach.

"He's chasing his hair!" Elizabeth cried.

"His beautiful blond locks!" yelped Jessica.

The twins burst out into a cataclysmic fit of laughter. They were laughing so hard that they had to hold on to each other for support. They rolled and shook, tears streaming down their faces. When one of them started to calm down, the other would start giggling, sending them both into a fresh round of laughter. Finally they sniffed and wiped their eyes, managing to settle down.

"Can you believe how hysterical the boys look dressed like cheerleaders?" said Jessica.

"It's a sight I thought I'd never see," said Elizabeth.

"Todd looks like a supermodel with his sleek brunette mane," said Jessica.

"And Ken looks like a Kewpie doll with those blond curls!" said Elizabeth. "He—"

Suddenly it struck Elizabeth that she and Jessica were talking again. Her voice trailed off as she realized that they were acting as if everything were normal. Both girls stopped talking and looked at each other. A moment of awkward silence followed.

Elizabeth cleared her throat. "Jess," she said in a heartfelt tone, "I'm so sorry about my date with Ken. Or, that is, your date." A crimson blush stained her cheeks. She took a deep breath and plunged ahead. "I had no intention of stealing your boyfriend. I was desperate to see how I really felt about him."

Elizabeth stole a look at her sister. Jessica was listening patiently. "I'm not trying to justify my actions," Elizabeth continued. "I know I was wrong to pull a twin switch, and I'm sorry." Elizabeth's lip trembled. "I found out that I didn't have feelings for Ken after all, but the price was too high." Elizabeth bit her lip and tears sprang to her eyes. "You're my soul mate, Jess, and I'm lost without you."

Elizabeth broke out in sobs, and Jessica grabbed her in a bear hug. "You're my soul mate too, Liz," she said. She grinned and looked up at her sister. "And after blackmailing you I deserved to be tricked."

Elizabeth sniffed and smiled between her tears. "That's true," she said, wiping away her tears with the back of her hand. "You deserved that and

164

more!" Then her expression became serious again. "You know, the worst of it all wasn't that I lost my boyfriend, but that I lost my sister."

"Of course you didn't lose me, silly," said Jessica. "You could never lose me." She slung an arm around her sister's waist. "And from the looks of Todd, it seems like you haven't lost him either."

"What do you mean?" Elizabeth asked.

"Well, he's obviously here to win you back," said Jessica.

Elizabeth shook her head sadly. "No, he's not. Jess, he won't have anything to do with me. I tried to talk to him before we left, but he wouldn't even listen to me. He's just here to keep Ken company."

"Elizabeth Wakefield," said Jessica, "sometimes you can be even more stubborn than me. Do you really think Todd would come all the way to Yosemite just for the ride?"

Elizabeth looked hopeful. "I—I guess not," she said.

"Liz, really," Jessica went on. "How many boyfriends would get dressed up as pom-pom girls just to keep their friends company?"

"Not too many," said Elizabeth with a laugh. "I guess you're right. Maybe he does want to make up after all."

"So are we going to put them out of their misery?" Jessica asked.

Elizabeth thought a moment. Then a mischievous look came into her eyes. "Yeees . . . but maybe not right away."

Jessica nodded as if reading her sister's thoughts.

"We should probably make their misery a little more acute first," she said.

"Hmm, let's see," said Elizabeth. "The guys have said that they're from Saskatchewan, Canada."

"And that they're just here to observe," added Jessica.

"Well, I think it's time the girls from Saskatchewan showed us their stuff," said Elizabeth, a wicked glint in her eye.

Chapter 13

"Wow, they look great," breathed Lila on Monday morning in the auditorium as they watched the Riverdale squad perform a fifties number set to the tune of "At the Hop."

"Neat costumes," said Jade Wu admiringly. "They look like they're at a sock hop." The girls were decked out in full fifties attire, wearing bobby socks and saddle shoes and letter sweaters with big *R*'s on them. They all had flippy ponytails tied high up on their heads.

It was the grand finale, the event that could change the competition. The ACA had gone all out for the affair. The band was sitting in the orchestra pit, breaking out into lively tunes between performances. Helium balloons were tied to the chairs and flapped gaily in the air. Colorful streamers adorned the walls.

Counting for one third of the total score, the

grand finale was the most important event of the competition, and the Sweet Valley High squad was prepared. They'd been on the lookout for foul play all day, and their fancy lace-trimmed uniforms were in perfect condition. They had locked them up in Lila's footlocker, where nobody could touch them.

"They're the best squad so far," whispered Amy to Lila as the Riverdale squad moved into position for the final segment of their program. "Rockin' and reelin', Riverdale's a-stealin'," sang the girls, twisting and whirling in pairs. "At the hop—bop bop. At the hop—bop bop."

"I can't believe how good they are," said Lila, suddenly overcome with doubt about their ability to win. She felt butterflies dancing around in her stomach, and her tongue went dry. They'd been sitting in the auditorium for hours, watching as one squad after another performed. The teams were pulling out all the stops for the grand finale, and each squad seemed better than the last.

"Don't worry," said Jessica reassuringly, twisting around to face them. "Their routine is fun and bouncy, but it lacks technical skill."

Jessica had a point. The girls were dancing and shaking more than they were jumping. "You're right," Lila agreed. "They're all show and no substance."

Lila was glad to see Jessica and Elizabeth back together again. The twins were sitting close together one rung below them, squeezing their hands together for support.

"It looks like our little scheme worked," whispered Lila to Amy, referring to their plan to force the girls together the day before. The entire squad had run off immediately following the final competition, leaving only Jessica and Elizabeth in their section of the bleachers. Lila and Amy had figured the twins would have to talk to each other if they were alone together. "It's good to see them back together again," agreed Amy with a satisfied smile. "Oh, look, the Reno squad is starting," she said nervously, turning her attention back to the floor. "And then it's our turn."

The Reno squad lined up on the floor, looking sharp and polished in crisp green-and-white uniforms. Lead by Marissa James, they began with an upbeat number that got the whole crowd moving.

Lila bit her lip as the Reno squad moved into position for the athletic part of their program. In pairs the girls stepped forward and executed impressive jump combinations. The crowd yelled as the last pair hopped back into line. One by one the girls shot up and landed in side-by-side splits, thrusting their green-and-white pom-poms up in the air. The crowd applauded heartily.

"You know, it really burns me up that they're doing so well," said Amy, gritting her teeth.

"I know," said Lila with venom in her voice. "It just doesn't seem right." Lila's jaw set in determination. "Well, we're going to knock them right out of the competition. And we're going to put

Marissa James and her scheming squad in their place."

Lila was surprised at the depth of her emotion. She had never realized cheerleading could be such a sophisticated activity. She had always found it to be a little gauche—a bunch of girls in tacky uniforms yelling out school-spirit cheers. When Lila had quit the squad ages ago, she had vowed never to cheer again. She had agreed to join Jessica's squad only in order to give her support. But with their chic uniforms and jazzy dance moves, the Sweet Valley squad had brought a whole new dimension to cheerleading.

"Check out the timing on that double wave!" said Amy, watching in awe as the Reno squad performed a double sequence of back crunches in perfect succession. "Now I know why it's called a wave."

Lila turned her attention back to the squad. They finished their routine with a splash, landing in a circle in Chinese splits and sweeping the floor from side to side with their pom-poms. "Wow, that's a really cool move," said Lila.

"It's neat, but kind of bizarre," put in Jessica. "I mean, it doesn't take much skill to wipe the floor."

"This is it," said Amy, putting a hand to her stomach as she noticed the Reno squad trotting off the stage. "We're up next."

The announcer's voice boomed over the loudspeaker. "And for the final squad in the final competition of the Tenth Annual ACA National Competition—Sweet Valley High!"

All the girls moved to jump up, but Jessica motioned for them to remain sitting. "Don't go on yet," Jessica said to the girls. "We've got a little surprise for you."

"Looks like the Wakefields are back in action," said Lila, grinning as Jessica and Elizabeth ran down the steps.

"What do you think they're going to do?" wondered Amy. "A special twin routine?"

"Maybe they're auditioning for a Doublemint commercial," joked Annie.

"What is this?" Heather snarled. "The Bobbsey twins make up, and they decide to steal the show?"

Lila watched with interest as Jessica and Elizabeth ran across the floor. The crowd applauded enthusiastically at the sight of the popular twins. With their beautiful matching red-and-white uniforms and shining golden-blond hair, they made a stunning pair.

Jessica leaned into the microphone, waiting for the crowd to quiet down. "We'd like to announce that we have a special treat for you today," said Jessica, grinning broadly.

Elizabeth spoke into the mike. "I think we've all been a little curious about the girls from Saskatchewan." The crowd stomped their feet in agreement, hooting and whistling.

"And we thought it was a shame for them to come all the way here from Canada without taking part in the festivities," added Jessica, leaning into the mike.

"So we're happy to announce that the Saskatchewan three have agreed to introduce our act with a little number of their own!" finished Elizabeth. She waved a tape in the air. "Please give them a warm welcome!"

Jessica and Elizabeth bounced off the stage, running up to the sound booth in the back of the auditorium to drop off the tape.

"Oh-mi-god," said Maria, clapping a hand over her mouth.

"They didn't!" said Amy.

"They did!" said Lila.

The audience went wild, hooting and screaming.

"Bring on the big girls!" somebody yelled.

"Let's see the Canadians move!" somebody else shouted.

"That's us!" said Ken, a horrified look on his face.

"But it can't be!" Todd said, scanning the crowds wildly for another Canadian squad.

"It is," Winston moaned, holding his head between his hands.

Ken stood up and gestured wildly to the crowd, signaling "no" by waving his arms across his face.

Todd stood up with him. "Sorry!" he mouthed to the crowd, waving like a movie star and blowing kisses. They both sat down.

"Sas-katch-ewan! Sas-katch-ewan!" clapped the audience in a cheer led by the Sweet Valley cheer-

172

leaders. "We want you on! We want you on!"

The crowd around them hustled them up, chanting and clapping the whole time.

"How could Maria betray me like this?" whimpered Winston as he was pulled to his feet with Todd and Ken.

As they stood up, they were greeted by thunderous applause and virtually pushed down the aisle.

"Well, girls," said Ken, linking arms with the two of them as they made their way to the stage, "looks like it's time for a little cheering."

"This is pushing the limits of friendship too far," said Winston, mortified.

"Don't worry, Winston," Todd said, trying to calm him. "Just follow me."

The boys trotted across the floor, smiling and waving at the audience. Todd racked his brains as they made their way to the stage, desperately trying to come up with a cheer.

"Start with the 'Be Aggressive' cheer," he hissed to the others as they reached the center of the stage. They'd heard the cheer enough, thought Todd. They ought to be able to remember the words.

The boys lined up with Todd in the middle and faced the audience. Todd gulped as he took in the masses in front of him. The auditorium was bursting with cheerleaders and fans. The judges sat in a row in front, staring up at them ominously. Bulbs flashed as members of the press took pictures.

"Oh, jeez, we're going to make the front page," groaned Winston.

Suddenly rock music began blaring through the loudspeaker. Todd took a deep breath. "Be aggressive! Be, be aggressive!" he shouted in time with the music, raising his voice an octave. He clapped his hands together and waved his hips from side to side.

"Be aggressive! Be, be aggressive!" joined in Ken and Winston in high voices, shaking their hips along with Todd and bumping them together. The crowd laughed with delight.

Todd rolled his wrists around each other in front of his body, lifting his right arm into the air and then his left. Winston and Ken watched him out of the corners of their eyes, following along with the motion. "C-A-N-A-D-A, we're gonna blow you a-way!" shouted Todd.

"C-A-N-A-D-A, we're gonna blow you a-way!" chorused Ken and Winston, imitating Todd's arm movements.

Todd put his arms above his head like a ballerina and began to whirl around in circles, Ken and Winston a step behind. The crowd laughed as they got a glimpse of the "girls'" muscular thighs.

"They love us!" Ken said as he began to execute his turn. "We're really pulling this off!"

"Whoa, it's slippery out here," muttered Todd under his breath as he suddenly twirled out of control, sliding to the ground. It seemed as if the surface of the floor was coated in some kind of oily substance.

"Yowee!" exclaimed Ken in the middle of a spin, his arms flailing out. Soon the three of them were on the ground together.

"OK, just act normal," whispered Todd. He jumped up quickly, balancing himself carefully on the slippery surface. Ken and Winston followed. Winston swayed dangerously from side to side, and Todd and Ken steadied him.

"Can-a-da! Can-a-da!" chanted Ken, taking over. He jumped into the air with one arm up and one leg out in an imitation of a herky. "Sis-boom-bah!" shouted Todd, jumping into the air after him. "Rah rah rah!" yelled Winston, flinging his arms and legs out wildly and hurtling into the air. Their legs went out from underneath them as they landed on the slimy surface, and the three of them went sliding wildly across the oily ground.

"Looks like the crowd's enjoying the show, huh?" said Elizabeth, her eyes glittering.

"Definitely," Jessica agreed. "Particularly our squad." The girls from the Sweet Valley squad seemed more amused than anyone else at the hysterical display of ineptitude on the stage. Maria was holding on to her stomach as if in pain, choking with laughter as she watched Winston dance awkwardly around the stage; Sandy and Jean were laughing so hard that tears were streaming down their faces; Lila and Amy were holding on to each other for support; Jade, Patty, and Sara were stomping their feet on the bleachers, chanting along with the boys.

Jessica, however, was eyeing the stage suspiciously. She had expected the boys to be clumsy, but she hadn't expected them to be flying all over the place. She squinted and peered at the stage. From the way the boys were slipping and sliding, it seemed as if there was some kind of oily slime covering the floor. Oily slime that had obviously been meant for the Sweet Valley team—compliments of Marissa and her crew.

Jessica turned and whispered into her sister's ear, "Have you noticed that the boys seem to be sliding around a lot?"

"Yeah," Elizabeth whispered back. "It looks like the stage is slippery." Suddenly she caught on to Jessica's line of thinking. She looked at her sister quickly. "You think—?"

Jessica nodded. "Marissa," she said.

"C'mon!" Elizabeth said. "Let's go find the referee."

"Be aggressive!" yelled Todd, scrambling up again. He loosened the heels of his sneakers and flung off his Keds, hoping to grip the floor better without his shoes on. "Be, be aggressive!" shouted Ken and Winston, flipping their shoes off as well.

"Take it off! Take it off!" yelled the crowds, clapping in time with the music. "Follow me," Todd said, out of breath. Barefoot, he put his arms out in front of him and flipped across the stage in a series of crooked cartwheels. Ken followed right behind.

Winston just watched, a stunned expression on his face. "C'mon, Winston," Todd hissed.

"Oh, boy," Winston said, steadying his gangly frame for the move. He sprang into the air, his long arms and legs flying in all directions as he attempted a cartwheel. He landed in a somersault and careened across the stage. His wig flew off in the opposite direction. The crowd roared with delight, thinking it was a gag.

"Oh, no!" Winston exclaimed, scrambling across the floor after it. He picked it up and frantically placed it back on his head. The wig was backward, and a sheath of red hair covered Winston's face. Winston coughed and quickly turned it around.

The crowd was in hysterics at this point, laughing and stamping their feet.

"Can-a-da!" yelled Todd, putting his hands on his hips and shaking his hips from side to side with each syllable. He held the position, his left hip stuck out dramatically.

"Sis-boom-bah!" shouted Winston, pumping his arms out in front of him like a monkey and holding the pose.

"Rah-rah-rah!" yelled Ken, turning around and wiggling his rear.

"Oh, no!" hissed Todd to the others. "Here comes Ms. Balsam."

"And an army of directors," said Ken, turning around. Ms. Balsam was marching down the aisle with a fierce look on her face, a bevy of directors close behind. They were clearly distraught to

177

have discovered an invasion of boys in their midst.

"Let's get out of here!" said Winston.

"Thank you, thank you!" yelled the boys in falsetto voices. They curtsied and ran off the stage.

"It's that squad over there," said Jessica to the referee, "the girls in the green-and-white uniforms." Jessica and Elizabeth were walking with the referee toward the Reno squad. He was a burly man dressed in a black-and-white uniform. They had found him sitting by the judges' boxes and had notified him of their suspicions. He had seemed a bit dubious but had agreed to check out the situation.

"What if we made a mistake?" chattered Elizabeth nervously as they approached the Nevada section of the audience. "What if they didn't do it? What if there's nothing on the court after all?"

"Liz, don't worry," Jessica said. Jessica didn't have a doubt in her mind that Marissa's squad was responsible for the oil on the floor. And when they reached the Reno section, she was sure of it. The Reno squad was the only group in the entire auditorium that wasn't laughing. The girls were staring at the stage in consternation, their mouths hanging open. Marissa James sat in the middle of the group. She was wound up like a top and wore a fierce expression on her face.

"Excuse me," said the guard, taking a seat with the group. "Who's the captain of this squad?" Jessica and Elizabeth stood back a few feet.

"I am," asserted Marissa, sitting up straight. "I'm Marissa James."

"If you don't mind, I'd like to have a look at your equipment," the referee said, indicating the large black duffel bag sitting at her feet.

"But whatever for?" asked Marissa, the picture of innocence. Suddenly she caught sight of Jessica and Elizabeth. She locked gazes with Jessica and her eyes narrowed.

"It looks like there's been some foul play on the stage, and we'd like to find out who's responsible," said the guard.

"Well, we don't know what you're talking about, do we, girls?" said Marissa defensively. The girls all shook their heads.

"Open the bag, please," said the referee calmly.

"But—but this is an outrage!" sputtered Marissa. "How dare you accuse our squad of—"

"Look, Miss James," interrupted the referee, "nobody's accusing you of anything. This is a routine process. We're going to check everybody's equipment until we find the guilty party."

"Well, we refuse," said Marissa hotly. "This bag is our private property, and you have no right to inspect it." Marissa folded her arms over her chest stubbornly.

"Yeah, we're not going to reveal the contents of our equipment bag to anybody without a search warrant," chimed in one of the squad members.

"Sorry, but it doesn't work that way," said the referee. "The ACA has conferred on me full privileges to search the equipment of any team when I deem it necessary." His tone turned menacing. "And I do indeed deem it necessary." He looked at Marissa for consent, but she just stared back at him defiantly.

"It looks like I'm going to have to confiscate the bag," said the referee with a sigh, grabbing the bag from the floor and hauling it onto the bench. Marissa's face burned scarlet as the referee unzipped the bag and rifled through it.

Jessica and Elizabeth gasped as he pulled out a case of baby oil. There were twenty-four bottles in all, and they were all empty. Jessica noticed that each bottle had a small elastic band attached to it—a band that would attach easily to the handle of a pom-pom.

Jessica leaned over to her sister and whispered into her ear. "So that's why the Reno squad swept the floor with their pom-poms at the end of their routine!" she said. "I thought that was a strange move!"

"Looks a little suspicious," said the referee, turning the case around as he examined the bottles. He put his finger along the rim of one of the bottles, then rubbed the oil between his fingers.

"We were suntanning earlier," said Marissa quickly. "And we used up all the oil."

"You don't look like you've got a lot of color," said the referee.

"Well, is it our fault if we don't tan well?" asked Marissa huffily.

"And may I ask what these little elastic straps

are for?" asked the referee, inspecting the bands.

"They're easier to carry that way," said Marissa smoothly.

"Oh, Marissa, what's the use?" said another girl on the team. "They're just going to check the stage. We might as well admit it."

"Look, he's holding a conference," said Jessica to Elizabeth as they made their way back to their seats. She pointed to the front of the room. It looked as if the referee was conferring with the directors of the ACA. Ms. Balsam looked agitated. She was standing up, waving her arms about. The crowd was murmuring restlessly, wondering what was causing the delay.

"What's going on?" asked Lila. "What were you doing over at Marissa's squad?"

"And why did you get the ref?" asked Maria eagerly.

Jessica and Elizabeth quickly filled the girls in on the latest events. "And so they covered the floor with baby oil at the end of their routine," finished Jessica.

"Oil that was meant for us," added Elizabeth.

"I can't believe it!" Annie said, outraged. "Of all the low-down stunts!"

"It doesn't surprise me in the slightest," said Heather. "I wouldn't put anything past Marissa James and her squad."

"Well, it looks like they're going to get their comeuppance now," said Maria in satisfaction.

"Hey, what happened to the boys?" asked

Jessica, looking up at the stage. The floor was empty, and the curtains were closed.

"They were officially escorted off the grounds by some of the directors," said Lila.

"You should have seen poor Winston's face!" said Maria with a giggle. "He looked like he thought he was going to be put away for life!"

Just then Zoe Balsam and the referee climbed the steps to the stage and disappeared behind the curtain.

"They must be checking the floor!" said Sara.

"And hopefully cleaning it!" added Jeanie.

Minutes later the curtains opened and Ms. Balsam took the mike.

"This is it," whispered Jessica excitedly. "Say good-bye to the Reno squad."

"I'd like to apologize for the delay," said Ms. Balsam. "We've had a few, er, technical difficulties. But everything's in order now, and we're ready to continue with the final performance of the competition. So please give a warm round of applause to the squad from Sweet Valley, California!"

The girls jumped up as the crowd cheered. Elizabeth leaned over to Jessica, concern in her eyes. "She didn't mention the Reno squad!" she said. "What do you think that means?"

"I don't know," said Jessica worriedly, "but it doesn't look good."

With Jessica at the lead the Sweet Valley High squad bounced onto the stage and took their positions for their final routine. The girls stood readied in a V formation, with one side dressed in all red and the other in all white. The floor had been cleaned up, and the audience was eager for the final performance to begin. The crowd murmured appreciatively as they took in the fancy outfits of the squad.

"Let's blow 'em out of their seats, guys!" said Jessica, smiling at her team. As the music started, the girls launched into their final and most difficult routine. "We got the fever, we're hot, we can't be stopped!" they sang out, performing an intricate medley of dance steps, athletic jumps, and fancy footwork. The girls had never performed better, thought Jessica with satisfaction. They looked tight and professional, as if they had been working together for years.

As the last beat of the music sounded, the girls jumped into position for their final pyramid. They quickly hoisted each other onto their shoulders, forming an impressive four-tiered standing pyramid. Sitting at the top, Jade raised her pom-poms victoriously into the air. The crowd gasped audibly as they observed the unprecedented feat.

While the girls held their positions, Jessica and Heather launched into a spectacular jump combination. Standing opposite one another, they broke into a series of front and back flips, finishing off with triple herkies and a trojan-jump combination. Not a step was out of place as the girls moved in unison through the difficult combination. Jessica and Heather leaped into the air and came down in side-by-side splits in front of the pyramid, raising their pom-poms in the air and smiling triumphantly.

The din of the audience was deafening. "Bravo! Bravo!" called the crowd, throwing streamers and confetti. A tissue-wrapped bouquet of roses landed on the stage.

A few minutes later the girls were back in their seats, breathing heavily and waiting anxiously for the results of the grand finale to be revealed. The entire audience was abuzz, chattering nervously among themselves as the final scores were tabulated. The announcer appeared on the stage and tapped on the mike, signaling for the crowd to quiet down.

Clutching the flowers in her arms, Jessica turned to Elizabeth anxiously. "Tell me when it's over!" she said, covering her ears with her hands and burying her head in her arms. At the sound of clapping she didn't look up, afraid that her team had been mentioned.

"Jess," said Elizabeth, nudging her on the shoulder. "You've got to listen! They're about to announce the second-place winners for this round!"

Jessica warily lifted her hands and grabbed on to Elizabeth for support. "What if they didn't disqualify the Reno squad?" she said. "What if they win instead of us?"

"That's impossible," Elizabeth reassured her.

"And now for our second-place grand-finale winners," boomed the announcer from the stage.

"Please give a hand to the girls from Sweet Valley, California!"

Jessica's face fell. "We didn't win," she said in an unbelieving tone. "We didn't win." She looked over at Patty. "Do we still have a chance?"

Patty shook her head sadly. "I don't think so. It looks like we're out of the running for good."

Jessica stared dejectedly at the bleachers, hugging her knees to her chest. They had come so close. So close. And now it was all over.

"And the first-place prize for the grand finale goes to the squad from Reno, Nevada!" boomed the announcer's voice.

The Reno squad let out an enthusiastic shout. Jessica looked over at the girls on the Reno squad. They were all crowded around Marissa, hugging and yelling. Jessica felt like pulling her hair out. Not only had they lost out on first place, but they had lost to the Reno squad. "I can't believe it!" she exclaimed in disgust. "They didn't penalize them at all."

"I guess they figured we got to compete fairly after all," Elizabeth said. She shook her head. "It just doesn't seem right."

"I think . . . I am going . . . to scream," muttered Heather through clenched teeth from the row behind them.

Just then Zoe Balsam walked across the stage and took the mike. "If you'll please settle down, I have an important announcement to make."

Jessica grabbed on to Elizabeth. "Do you think—?" she asked.

"Let's hope so," Elizabeth said, holding up crossed fingers.

The audience quieted down, and Ms. Balsam cleared her throat. "I have some very unfortunate news. Before the final performance we discovered that somebody had tampered with the stage in an attempt to sabotage the competition," she said. "It appears that the squad from Reno, Nevada, is responsible for the damage."

A murmur rose from the crowd. Ms. Balsam held up a hand for silence. "I have discussed the situation with the other directors of the American Cheerleading Association. The Reno squad is hereby officially disqualified from the competition and from the ACA. Thank you," she said. The crowd chattered noisily as Ms. Balsam walked off the court.

The announcer took the mike again. "So congratulations to Sweet Valley High for winning the grand finale!"

Jessica fell back in her seat, weak with relief. She looked around at her team, her eyes shining with pride. The girls seemed moved. Some of them were laughing, and some of them were crying. They had really done it. They had taken first place for four competitions in a row.

The band struck up a chord while the officials prepared for the awards ceremony. The girls whispered excitedly among themselves while they waited.

"Patty, what does this mean?" asked Amy excitedly.

Patty was busy doing calculations. "I'm not really sure," she said, looking in confusion at the rows of numbers covering the page, "but I think it looks good."

"Ladies and gentlemen, please take your seats," boomed Zoe Balsam from the podium. "I am happy to welcome you to the awards ceremony of the Tenth Annual National Competition."

Elizabeth squeezed Jessica's hand as Ms. Balsam began. Jessica looked over at her with a happy smile, confident that they would place.

"The third-place prize goes to a squad whose jumps, stunts, and combinations have entertained and impressed us all this weekend. Please give a round of applause to the Texas Tigers from San Antonio, Texas!" The crowd clapped enthusiastically as the captain of the San Antonio squad ran onto the court to accept the bronze trophy. She made a short speech at the podium and ran off with her trophy, waving it in the air happily.

Jessica held her breath as Ms. Balsam continued. "And our second-place prize marks a landmark event," she said, smiling at the crowd. "For the first time in the history of the competition, we have witnessed a team move from last place to second. So, for the squad that has made an amazing comeback and has stunned us all with their originality, energy, and skill, I'm thrilled to award the second-place prize to Sweet Valley High from Sweet Valley, California!"

The squad erupted with joy, jumping up and

down and hugging each other. Lightbulbs flashed in their faces as Heather and Jessica ran down to the stage together to accept the big silver trophy Ms. Balsam was holding out.

Heather took the mike. "I'd just like to say that I've competed in nationals before, but I've never encountered a more talented group of teams. So on behalf of our squad, we'd like to thank all the teams that have competed this weekend for making this such an exciting competition." All the squads cheered. "Thanks to the Braselton Bulldogs for being such terrific cabinmates!" The Alabama squad let out a shout. "And to the Reno squad as well—for making this such an, er, memorable experience!" The audience laughed. "And finally we'd like to express our appreciation to the ACA for making it all happen."

Jessica leaned into the mike. "And most of all, we'd like to thank the Sweet Valley High *boys'* cheerleading squad for their valiant attempt at cheerleading. I think they've made us all realize just what a difficult sport it is." The crowd went wild, whistling and yelling catcalls. "Todd, Ken, and Winston, we couldn't have done it without you!" She and Heather raised the trophy in the air, both holding on to one side.

"We did it!" said Jessica gleefully as she and Heather walked across the stage.

"See, Jessica," Heather said, holding the trophy to the light and admiring it. "Aren't you happy I came to Sweet Valley? Aren't you glad I agreed to stay on the squad? You never would have won without me."

I can't believe I let her back in, thought Jessica, rolling her eyes heavenward and smiling to herself. It looked as if Heather would always be Heather.

Chapter 14

"I think that was the most exciting weekend of my entire life!" exclaimed Maria, walking arm in arm with Elizabeth toward the parking lot of the cheerleading compound on Monday.

"Definitely," agreed Elizabeth. *A little* too *exciting,* she thought. She had enjoyed herself more than she had expected to, but she was glad that the weekend's festivities were finally over. The girls had packed up their gear and said good-bye to the girls from Alabama. The Alabama squad had done extremely well, placing fifth overall. "We'll see y'all next year!" Wilhemina had said. "You better watch out, though!" added Peggy May. "We're gonna be tough competition next year!"

The rest of the girls followed behind them, walking in groups and chattering happily. Still wearing their grand-finale cheerleading outfits, they were carrying duffel bags stuffed with clothing and equipment.

Heather brought up the rear, carrying nothing but the silver trophy, which she was treating like a prized possession.

Elizabeth pushed open the gate and walked into the lot. Suddenly she stopped in her tracks as she caught sight of Todd, looking clean and handsome in the sparkling sunlight. Todd and Winston were waiting for the girls outside the gates, dressed in normal clothing again.

"Winston!" Maria exclaimed, running up to the boys. "I almost didn't recognize you!" Elizabeth followed slowly behind, her heart pounding loudly in her chest. Jessica had convinced her that Todd was ready to forgive her, but now she was filled with doubts again. What if he still wouldn't talk to her?

Winston leaned against Todd's black BMW, folding his arms across his chest. "Girls, I will never forgive you," he said in mock anger. "How could you do that to us?"

"That was cruel and unusual punishment," Todd agreed.

"Winston, we just couldn't resist it," Elizabeth said, making a sorry face.

"You couldn't resist it!" Winston yelped.

"Well, you have to admit it was a once-in-a-lifetime opportunity," said Maria. "It's not often that you guys dress up in purple-and-yellow cheerleading uniforms. A performance was definitely in order." Maria looked up at Winston, her warm brown eyes laughing.

"Hmmph," Winston pouted, looking away.

191

Maria reached out a hand. "C'mon, Win, you guys looked great out there! You were the highlight of the competition," she said.

"We certainly were!" said Winston. "I never realized what kind of cheerleading talents I had." He pulled Maria toward him in a hug. Then he held her back at arm's length. "But don't you dare ever do anything like that again!" he warned. Maria laughed and snuggled up to him.

Todd and Elizabeth stood by their side, shuffling their feet uncomfortably and looking at the ground. Elizabeth glanced up at Todd shyly, and he gestured for her to step away. They walked a few moments in silence, sitting down in a grassy spot by the parking lot.

"Cruel and unusual punishment?" asked Elizabeth, picking at a piece of grass.

"Well, unusual, but maybe not cruel," said Todd. "I guess I deserved it."

"Does that mean you forgive me?" asked Elizabeth, a hopeful look on her face.

"Liz, I *do* forgive you," Todd said in an earnest voice. He took her hand. "I forgave you right away. I guess I just didn't want you to know it. I was so hurt, and—"

"Oh, Todd!" Elizabeth interrupted, tears springing to her eyes. "I'm so sorry! You're the last person in the world I wanted to hurt."

Todd gently wiped away a tear as it trickled down Elizabeth's cheek.

"Are those tears of sorrow or happiness?" he asked.

"I think both," said Elizabeth, starting to cry for real. Todd grabbed her in his arms and held her in a bear hug.

Elizabeth leaned into his arms, feeling the heat of his body envelop her. Her whole body relaxed. "Oh, Todd, I missed you so much," she said. "And I thought I'd lost you for good."

"You could never lose me, Liz," said Todd, his voice low and husky. "I'm with you now, and forever."

Elizabeth's heart skipped a beat, and she lifted her face to his. Todd leaned down and hungrily caught her lips, kissing her fervently.

Elizabeth smiled up at Todd when they pulled away. "You know what I missed most?" she said.

"What?" Todd asked, wrapping an arm around her.

"The little things," Elizabeth said. "Like talking on the phone and walking down the hall together and going to the Dairi Burger—"

"Well, we're going to have to get home so we can start making up for lost time," said Todd. "And I think the Dairi Burger is our first priority."

"Hey, y'all!" yelled a girl's voice. Elizabeth looked up to see Wilhemina and Peggy May bounding toward them.

"Sorry, are we interruptin' somethin'?" asked Peggy May with a twinkle in her eye as they approached the two sitting on the grass.

"No, no," said Elizabeth, laughing. She quickly introduced Todd to the girls.

"I thought you two had already left!" said Elizabeth with surprise.

"The bus is just getting ready to go," said Peggy May.

"Hey, you're the guy in the picture!" said Wilhemina. "I knew you two looked like you belonged together."

Peggy May looked at him strangely. "Haven't I seen you somewhere before?" she asked, looking Todd over carefully.

Todd's face turned beet-red. "Uh, I don't think so," he said.

"It must have been the picture," said Elizabeth, her eyes dancing merrily.

"Well, we've gotta go now," said Wilhemina. "You take good care of yourself, Liz. We're gonna miss you."

"I'm going to miss you too," said Elizabeth, leaning in to give both girls a hug.

"See y'all next year!" said Peggy May, waving as they walked away.

"Did you hear what Wilhemina said?" asked Elizabeth, taking Todd's hand. "We look like we belong together."

"That's because we *do* belong together," said Todd with a smile, kissing her gently on the cheek. They walked hand in hand back to the parking lot, smiling happily. They found Maria waiting by Todd's car. Winston had settled into the driver's seat. His eyes were closed and he was snoring lightly. He was clearly exhausted from his weekend spent dressing and acting like a cheerleader.

"Hey, Winston, you driving?" said Todd, opening the front door of his BMW. "Rah, rah, rah!"

Winston said, opening his eyes with a start. Laughing, Elizabeth jumped into the passenger seat and Maria hopped in back.

"I said, are you driving?" Todd repeated.

"No way, man, you're the chauffeur," said Winston, now fully awake. He clambered over the front seat and tumbled awkwardly into the back of the car, a pile of gangly legs and arms.

"Winston, it looks like you could still use a few cheerleading lessons," teased Maria as Winston scampered into an upright position, breathing hard.

"No way," said Winston, sitting back in the seat. "My cheerleading days are over!"

"Hey, Liz, is that you?" asked Ken as Jessica headed for the bus.

Jessica wheeled around, her eyes flaming as she recognized Ken's voice. Again! He had mistaken her again! And she was dressed in regular clothes with her hair down.

"I can't believe you—" began Jessica hotly; then she stopped as she looked into Ken's crinkly bright-blue eyes. He was only teasing her, she realized.

"Jessica, I promise I'll never confuse you with your twin sister again," Ken said in an imploring tone. He looked up at her with an incredibly sweet expression on his handsome face. Jessica could feel her heart melt.

"And I promise I'll never make you cheer in public again," answered Jessica with a smile. "But I kind of like you in a skirt."

"I like you in a skirt, too," said Ken, pulling her toward him. He wrapped his arms around her and hugged her to him. "Oh, Jess, I missed you," Ken whispered in her ear, nibbling on her earlobe. He dropped feather-light kisses on her ear, traveling along her neck until he reached her lips. He kissed her softly, tenderly, then more and more urgently until they were wrapped in a passionate embrace.

Just then a car passed, honking loudly.

Jessica pulled away from Ken, feeling a little dazed. She blinked and looked up. Todd and Elizabeth were driving by in Todd's BMW, with Winston and Maria in back.

"It looks like we're going to have to save this for a later date," said Ken with a grin.

"A lot of them," said Jessica happily, linking her arm through his.

"Bye-bye, Kendall!" Todd and Winston yelled, hanging out the windows and waving.

"Ta-ta, Tilda!" said Ken in a falsetto voice. "See you later, Winnie!" He blew them all a kiss. Todd honked his horn a few times and headed out of the parking lot, his purple-and-gold pom-poms floating off the back of the car.

"I guess it's the bus for us," said Ken, turning back to Jessica with a wry smile. "But first—" He pulled her toward him again and brought his lips to hers.

"Here's to our cocaptains!" shouted Maria, standing in the aisle as the bus pulled out of the parking lot. She raised a pom-pom in the air.

"To Jessica and Heather!" yelled Patty and Jade, waving their pom-poms wildly in the air.

"For bringing us to vic-tory!" added Sandy. All the girls let out a whoop and cheered. Jessica laughed in delight. She was seated in the middle of the bus with Ken, thrilled to be the center of attention with an adoring boy by her side. Ken wrapped an arm around her proudly and leaned in to kiss her on the cheek.

"Hey, hey, none of that," said Lila with a grin, sitting across from them with Amy.

"Yeah, keep it clean," said Amy. "This is a family show."

"Hey, Ken, what happened to your cheerleading outfit?" asked Annie, twisting around in her seat.

"Oh, I put it away for next year," Ken said good-naturedly.

"Are you going to join the squad?" asked Lila. "Tryouts are in the fall."

Ken looked as if he were considering the option, then shook his head. "I think I'm going to stick to football," he said. "It's less stressful."

"This *was* quite a nerve-racking competition!" exclaimed Jeanie.

"Yeah, I think the greatest challenge of all was dealing with Marissa James and her squad's tricks," said Heather.

"But we pulled it off," said Sara happily. "We went to nationals for the first time and we placed!"

"And next year we're going to win!" said Jessica. The bus driver honked the horn twice in agreement, and all the girls cheered.

Late that afternoon Todd deposited Elizabeth on her doorstep. She bounced up the walk cheerfully, breathing in the fresh, balmy air. Everything was back to normal again. She and Jessica were speaking once more, and she and Todd were back together again.

"Hey, Liz!" Jessica greeted her as she walked into the sunny Wakefield kitchen. Jessica was sitting at the butcher-block table with a lemonade, flipping through the latest version of Cheer Ahead. "I thought you would beat us back."

"We stopped at the Dairi Burger on the way home," said Elizabeth happily, opening the refrigerator and taking out a carton of orange juice. She was thrilled to have normalcy again—a conversation with Jessica, a kiss with Todd, a bite to eat at the Dairi Burger with friends. Elizabeth poured herself a glass and leaned against the counter, her legs crossed at the ankles.

Suddenly Jessica sucked in her breath as she turned the page. "Wow!" she breathed. "Hey, Liz, come look at this totally cool new uniform they've got in the catalog. It's like a jumpsuit, with suspenders."

"Uh, hold on a sec," said Elizabeth, looking down at the uniform she was still wearing and realizing that things weren't *quite* back to normal. Elizabeth downed her juice and ran upstairs.

Once in her room, Elizabeth ripped off her uniform and pulled on a pair of khaki shorts and a peach T-shirt. "That's more like it," she said out loud, happy to be back in regular clothes. Flinging her gym bag over her shoulder, she grabbed her journal and left the room.

Feeling like herself again, Elizabeth skipped down the steps and returned to the kitchen.

Dropping her journal onto the counter, Elizabeth reached into the gym bag and pulled out her folded uniform, holding it in her outstretched palms like a platter. "Here, Jess," Elizabeth said, ceremoniously presenting the outfit to her.

"But what's this?" Jessica said, her blue eyes wide.

"It was fun while it lasted," said Elizabeth, dropping the uniform onto the table, "but I officially resign." She pulled out her pom-poms and tossed them, one by one, on top of the pile.

"You mean I didn't convert you?" asked Jessica.

"Not by a long shot," Elizabeth said with a smile. She picked up her journal and sat down in a chair, chewing the edge of her pen thoughtfully. "But I sure did get lots of material to write about!"

Do you know where your mother is? Don't miss the next Sweet Valley High Super Thriller, **Murder in Paradise,** *when Alice Wakefield takes the twins to a luxurious spa and then mysteriously disappears!*

Bantam Books in the Sweet Valley High series
Ask your bookseller for the books you have missed

SIGN UP FOR THE SWEET VALLEY HIGH® FAN CLUB!

Hey, girls! Get all the gossip on Sweet Valley High's® most popular teenagers when you join our fantastic Fan Club! As a member, you'll get all of this really cool stuff:

- Membership Card with your own personal Fan Club ID number
- A Sweet Valley High® Secret Treasure Box
- Sweet Valley High® Stationery
- Official Fan Club Pencil (for secret note writing!)
- Three Bookmarks
- A "Members Only" Door Hanger
- Two Skeins of J. & P. Coats® Embroidery Floss with flower barrette instruction leaflet
- Two editions of *The Oracle* newsletter
- Plus exclusive Sweet Valley High® product offers, special savings, contests, and much more!

Be the first to find out what Jessica & Elizabeth Wakefield are up to by joining the Sweet Valley High® Fan Club for the one-year membership fee of only $6.25 each for U.S. residents, $8.25 for Canadian residents (U.S. currency). Includes shipping & handling.

Send a check or money order (do not send cash) made payable to "Sweet Valley High® Fan Club" along with this form to:

SWEET VALLEY HIGH® FAN CLUB, BOX 3919-B, SCHAUMBURG, IL 60168-3919

NAME _____
(Please print clearly)

ADDRESS _____

CITY_____ STATE _____ ZIP_____
(Required)

AGE _____ BIRTHDAY_____ /_____ /_____

Offer good while supplies last. Allow 6-8 weeks after check clearance for delivery. Addresses without ZIP codes cannot be honored. Offer good in USA & Canada only. Void where prohibited by law.
©1993 by Francine Pascal   LCI-1383-193